"These beautifully written and emotionally affecting
Texas stories deserve to be read widely."
—Leon Hale

"Hale shows a great respect for her characters and for
the difficulty of their deceptively ordered existence, as
well as for the problems they suffer because so much
cannot be spoken."
—Francine Prose

A Wall of Bright
Dead Feathers

A Wall of Bright Dead Feathers

STORIES

~~

Babette Fraser Hale

WINEDALE PUBLISHING
Houston / Winedale

Copyright © 2021 by Babette Fraser Hale
Printed in the United States of America

Library of Congress Cataloging-in-Publication Data
Fraser Hale, Babette, 1944-
A Wall of Bright Dead Feathers : stories / Babette Fraser Hale
p. cm.
I. Title

ISBN 978-0-9657468-9-2

Winedale Publishing
P.O. Box 77
Round Top, Texas 78954

For L.H.

Contents

A Wall of Bright Dead Feathers

Drouth

2011

Every day they pass the old farm, and every day Ro wonders if anyone lives there. The buildings show signs of desertion—the barn roof of rusty tin, the worn wood siding of the house, unpainted pickets on the fence. There are no hens, no cows, not even a cat skulking in the long dry grass clumped at the corners of the barn.

Then, one morning, she sees two old people working in the yard. The man, white-headed, pushes a hand tiller through soil as rich and black as fudge cake crumbles. The woman wears a sunbonnet, the pioneer kind that wraps around her face from the top and sides. It's a bleached white bonnet tied securely under her chin with a blue ribbon, and when she turns, her face inside it is a flower, round and bright.

"How old do you think they are?" Ro asks Cam, who's driving.

"Not as old as they look," he says.

But Ro's thinking they're like a man and woman from

the Thirties, maybe, when her grandfather's generation abandoned the farm for the city, and their parents, left behind, made do. Ro's mother would have said that the old couple had found a seam in time back then, and what Ro sees is their image leaking into the present like light around a door that doesn't quite fit.

This idea pleases Ro. She'd like to believe that nothing is ever really lost. It gives her a tipped, hopeful feeling.

2009

Cam is walking by the Serpentine in Hyde Park, London, when the call comes. It's one of those misted English days, not quite spring, when the trees in the park are fuzzed expectantly, as though someone has exhaled green smoke into the webbing of bare limbs.

A day like this makes him conscious of the poets who preceded him here, breathing a version of this air, smelling the moist, chill probability of the new season. Each step he takes places him among them, along a continuum of feet, of observation, too, trees, water, birds, people. The nearby traffic, whizzing along streets slick with rain-shine, doesn't dispel the sensation. All poets occupy their own time, but also this ribbon of connected time, leading forward into a world whose poetry cannot now be imagined, not its form nor its language and definitely not its content.

For an irrational moment, he feels exalted. He shouldn't be here at all, in London, on a Monday. He ought to be at school, working, and would be if he hadn't just spent the weekend here with Angelica, his tutor's wife. An altogether brilliant weekend, actually, and not the first, although it was the first time he'd been inside her house.

Cam stops briefly to examine the peculiar mossy clumps clotting the water's edge. Brownish tendrils trail beneath the gleaming surface for more than a few feet, reaching toward the invisibility of deeper pools.

Angelica calls her arrangement with Michael an open marriage and it suits Cam to believe her. If this were Texas, he might look at the situation more closely. He might have his doubts. He likes Michael. He wouldn't want to hurt him.

Cam's own circumstances are more sharply incised. He has a girl back home. (Doesn't everyone?) A girl, Rose, rooted in real life, no way a part of this dream, which is how he thinks of his time abroad, his fellowship. A time apart.

This kind of thinking allows the investigation of many desires. It allows construction of a Cameron who drains experience of every possibility, pouring it all into his work. He wishes it were true. Wishes the vessel into which he excretes (a more accurate image) were made of lasting material, gleaming surfaces.

Home's reality requires a different version of himself, a person who will chuck it all and go back, not for Ro, so much, but for Greg, his little brother, getting sicker every day.

His dad's been home—twice—hitching both times from Kabul on the company plane. But Ro and his mother are united in telling Cam to stay. "You'll be done in a month. There's nothing you can do here," Ro says.

He has accepted that. He would feel better about it, though, if he were less aware of how much he wants to finish out the fellowship, enjoy the perks of remaining—not just the long boozy discussions of craft, but the way their whole culture here values poetry. And then, of course, Angelica.

Cam stops to light a cigarette. Ro detests the habit, but people here still smoke. Angelica smokes. He looks out at the platinum sheen of the water, deserted still, too cold for boating. He has never rowed across it, never wanted to see from that closer perspective the detritus lying below.

It's then that his phone—unwelcome insect—buzzes against his thigh. Ro's words take only a few seconds and through them he stands without moving.

And then he does what he will always regret. He begins walking away. Away from the lake, the park, down Edinburgh Gate and across the Brompton Road, although he will never remember doing that—crossing, avoiding the cars, emerging on the other side unscathed, oblivious. He becomes aware of where he is halfway along Sloane Street, where Pont Street intersects. He has a moment then to change his mind, to hail a cab and begin the process of leaving—the train to Oxford, clothes, passport, airplane ticket—but he doesn't. Instead, he turns toward Pavilion Road, plods down it until he comes to the shiny red door of a tiny brown mews house. He pushes the button and hears the peremptory bleat somewhere deep inside.

Tears are coursing down his face by the time Angelica, still in her blue satin wrapper, opens the door.

2008

The plink of the aluminum bat—D sharp—brings Ro to her feet, but no worries, Greg's got it. Cam grins down at her as she resumes her seat. His thigh is warm and slightly sweaty against hers.

The seventh grade game on this overcast April Saturday has populated the stands around them with otherwise job-squeezed dads in full liberated voice. Greg's dad, Kevin, would be here, too, if Halliburton hadn't sent him to Afghanistan. The boys' mother, Linnie, works weekends selling houses, so Ro and Cam have child patrol for their Saturday entertainment.

Ro doesn't mind. She loves Greg. She feels an almost proprietary thrill when he fields a hot one—isn't that the term?—slings it accurately to first base. Baseball has expanded her vocabulary, previously far too bookish and riddled with the Italian words used in musical notation. Ro is a pianist, a promising one, according to her professors. She is less sure about that. Recitals make her conscious of her nerves like piano strings tuned sharp, well past the point of sweet balance if not quite yet to the snapping point.

The brothers are close despite the nine-year difference in age. Cam watches with admiration—and, Ro guesses, a little envy—as Greg executes maneuvers with a grace that Cam can't equal. Mainly, though, the boys share a love of words in serial stories they invent that never end. They'll do it in the car, picking up and expanding a thread from one day to another, while Ro listens. She feels privileged to have this glimpse into the male imagination, so different from her childhood world of pretty dolls, books and piano scales.

Greg illustrates the stories, tacks the pen and ink drawings on the walls of his room in between posters of his favorite athletes. He and Cam walk around reviewing the action, thinking of plot twists. Ro doesn't care for the level of bloodshed the tales require, but she likes to think Cam's tenderness with the boy shows what a good father he will be some day.

She and Cam have been a couple since the night her roommate dragged her to a poetry reading the second week of freshman year at Rice. Cam—only a sophomore, then—had reminded her of a blue heron when he stood. In faded denim, his tall, slightly stooped figure held that kind of stillness. Then he began to read and she noticed how the overhead light fell across the planes of his face, hooding his eyes so that he seemed exotic, almost foreign, and she began to listen.

2009

At noon on the third day after Greg's funeral, Ro is playing hostess at Cam's house, refreshing glasses of iced tea. Drop-ins have been gathering in the living room all week, often until nearly eight o'clock at night. But they're not the only ones. From the moment Greg died, volunteers from Linnie's church have been arriving in teams, like caterers with a specialty menu.

Today, Linnie is hunched on the sofa beside one of

them, a friend from Bible study. Both blonde heads bow to the older woman's inaudible murmur. Occasionally, one or the other will nod.

Ro knows very little about organized religion, since her parents weren't members of a church. She'd only been to services a couple of times, on the Sunday of a sleep-over with one or another friend. It didn't matter to her which denomination—Methodist, Baptist, Episcopalian (once)—she liked the music, the singing, the hymns. It seemed to her that's what everyone liked.

One day, she asked her father why their family didn't go and he said he'd been "churched out" as a kid. Too many forced revivals in the small west Texas town where he grew up. Her mother had a different reason. Fran had been raised a Catholic, and had fallen away in college over certain teachings and what she called "the thoughtless arrogance of sermons." When pressed, Fran would say that she felt more spiritually elevated in the Houston Arboretum, even with West Loop traffic whizzing by, than she ever had at Mass.

Around five o'clock, Dr. Bailey, Linnie's pastor, arrives. With the last finger sandwich in hand, he settles his large body into the green vinyl recliner that Cam's dad, Kevin, occupies when he's at home. Kevin, like Cam, missed the funeral, and he's expected on the weekend.

Ro can deal with that, but she wears the combined absence of Cam and Greg like an anvil, cold and very heavy, pulling at the center of her chest. Returning to the kitchen for more food, she is mildly surprised not to be tilted forward from the weight.

The door swings toward her, then, and Cam pushes through—unshaven, his fair hair matted, blue smudges beneath his eyes. The duffel over his shoulder collides with the corner of a cabinet, rattling the saucers.

Behind Ro, Linnie makes a choking sound. Her cheeks are dark and wet as she stumbles toward him. In the room that has grown silent, the smack of her slap is almost as shocking as the fact of it.

The pastor arrives at Linnie's side with surprising agility. His fingers indent the soft flesh of her bare upper arm, lightly, but she's not finished with her son. "How could you?" Her voice is low. "I told Greg you were coming, but you weren't, were you? You're selfish to the bone, Cameron. It's a terrible sin."

Cam's head droops like he's been hung by his collar on a hook.

But Ro knows the truth. Ro is the selfish one, not Cam. She kept telling him not to come. She wanted him to finish all the things he'd begun over there. Finish and be done with them.

The following days at Ro's small apartment disappear into a stream of movies, junk food, beer. Ro has never seen Cam drink so steadily. He stumbles on the steps and sleeps drenched in sour-smelling sweat.

She has taken a week's vacation from her music classes, claiming a death in the family, which is almost true. In the daytime, she leaves only to buy food, or meet with two after school students whose lessons she couldn't cancel. Whenever she tries to talk to Cam about his mother, about the strain Linnie's under, about how she hadn't really meant it, he burrows down further into the sofa. When Linnie calls, Ro is the one who receives her weepy apologies.

On Friday, the 4PM lesson stands her up and when Ro returns home, Finding Nemo is playing silently on the TV. Cam is in his usual spot, wrapped tightly in her ancient fraying quilt. She looks down on him for a moment, the question mark of his body under the quilt. And she remembers the college boy who slept after sex as if he'd landed in a heap at the bottom of a sharp incline. He had been sensitive then, too, but certain in the way he took the sound of language—not so different from music, after all—and used it to open her eyes. Less than two years ago, that's all it's been.

No point in waking him, she'll just go and grab a juice from the fridge. But her shoe, as she edges past, lands on something next to the old box she uses for a coffee table. The object, plastic, squirts away, bounces off a chair leg. A pill bottle. Empty.

Ro flings herself against Cam. He's breathing, barely. She gives him a good whack. Nothing. What kind of pills? But she's calling 9-1-1 before she even thinks to read the label.

2011

Ro and Cam have lived in central Texas since April. After his latest hospital stay—the third in two years—Cam wanted to get away from Houston and all of its associations. He needed to write something long, he said, prose. To do that, he wanted to be surrounded by birds and fresh air, not cars and smog.

There were no more poems.

"You can do composition, Ro," he said, persuading her. After all, her small inheritance would be paying the bills. She'd been talking about how she might try composing, now that recitals had become impossible.

Impossible is what she told him, anyway, although not on account of the nervousness she blamed. That had actually resolved easily enough with a beta blocker.

Her problem was that the music itself had become too much of a distraction. Performance, certainly, and teaching, too—she should never have left Cam alone that day in her apartment, the week after Greg died. She should have noticed how sick he was. She should have been paying attention.

Ro has always been accused of living in a dream world. Her mother was forever chasing her out of doors, off sofas, away from books and computers. Or enrolling her in drama class—to bring her "out of herself"—and ballet, where music became no more than background to any number of uncomfortable contortions. For Ro, only practicing the piano had been an acceptable retreat from the strain of engaging a world of people who had their own thoughts about her and what she needed, or what they needed from her.

Even practice asks too much now, though, with the way it swallows time. The early sun will be gilding the treetops when she sits down at the keyboard, and when she rises, the day itself has fallen off into the west.

Years can disappear like that. Your life can disappear.

Ro had turned sixteen the spring her father, Tom, disturbed the hive. He'd been on vacation that week, trimming dead wood out of a pecan tree near the garage. By the time her mother found him at the foot of the ladder, he was already dead. Anaphylactic shock, they said.

Ro, arriving home from school, had come upon Fran kneeling beside the body, white-faced and dry-eyed, lost in all practical ways from that moment forward.

Ro had been stubborn about it, though. She was determined that her mother would not only get better, but that whatever ailed her was simply a choice she made, a role she was playing. Ro refused to cooperate with that. She did no more of what she thought of as her mother's chores than were absolutely necessary and she did them wrapped in the protective dissonance of Schoenberg, music she normally hated. For weeks it must have seemed like she didn't remove her earbuds even to sleep.

Fran wasn't pretending, however. Within the year, she had exited decorously, with pills—leaving behind the safe deposit key and a note of polite regret to the daughter her husband had called his little prodigy.

People are so stupid, Ro told herself when adults kept saying how fortunate she was to have Aunt Helen nearby. Helen was her father's sister, a career woman, as they used to say. A nurse, the administrative kind. Aunt Helen regarded suicide as a topic to edge carefully around, even if that meant keeping your distance from the daughter abandoned so abruptly. Food, a roof, transportation, advice about colleges: all those things Helen could provide, and did, willingly.

There was no one, however, for Ro to talk to. No one to tell her it was perfectly natural for every orphan in every book she'd read to re-appear in the darkness before sleep each night, to be balanced carefully along a scale of ultimate desertion. There were plucky orphans, tragic ones, superheroes, and nowhere among them were parents who had died from an allergy to bees or an imbalance of neurochemicals. None of those orphans, therefore, wondered as Ro did, whether vulnerabilities, hidden weaknesses like that of the body or what is commonly called character, lay somewhere deep inside them, too.

Even before she met Cam, Ro suspected that music had become peripheral to what she really wanted, which was to be part of an intact family, one that wouldn't be gone overnight, snap, the way a lid shuts on a piano keyboard.

II.

2011

In the middle of that drouthy summer in the country, Ro and Cam are invited to a party at the local *shützenverein* hall where the largely German community gathers to shoot targets and socialize.

While Ro waits for Cam to find drinks, she admires the array of homemade food arranged on three long tables by the door. The wives that day have set out pickles and preserves of plums, figs, sour grapes, along with cakes for purchase—Red Velvet and German Chocolate—benefitting the upkeep of the hall.

"I know you," says one of the women sitting in a lazy circle of chairs beside the food. Ro has to look twice, but then she sees: It's the sunbonnet lady. Even without headgear, her face looks round as a melon sliced through.

"You're young Miz Maxwell that just moved into the old Tiedemann place." The black eyes are kind and missing little, Ro thinks, except the fact she's just Ro Weldon, the way she's always been.

"You should come to our church sometime. Our organ is famous, you know. It was made entirely made by hand, a very long time ago."

Ro's face grows warm with uncertainty. If this is an invitation to worship, that would be awkward since Cam is as anti-religion as her parents ever were. Or is it something to do with music?

The other women in the circle of chairs wait with polite interest for Ro to speak. Only the old lady beams at her like there is nothing more anyone needs to say.

The days they spend in the rented house move according to the rigid schedule Doctor Fulton recommends.

Ro cooks breakfast. Cam eats. Afterwards, he takes his computer into the tiny back room and remains there all morning with his door shut. He says he's writing, although Ro has seen no pages.

While he works, Ro confronts the rooms the way you

would an enemy. It isn't the house she hates so much, really, as the inescapable sifting of dust from the unpaved road that floats in every time a pickup or gravel truck goes by. She vacuums, wipes down furniture, even the walls, but the fine powder seems more resistant to her efforts every day.

Chores are like that for her, always rushing ahead on their own schedule of increase and complexity, refusing to cooperate. When she cleaned her room in college—not too often, it has to be said—she'd listen to Bach, a great striding fugue to carry her through. Here, though, she doesn't use her iPod for fear she might not hear Cam if he calls. Or miss the altered nature of the silence if he doesn't call. That is her greatest fear.

2008-9

Cam had been in England for just two months when Gregory's glioblastoma was diagnosed. Ro could hear his shock when they told him. The reception had been so clear, much clearer than an ordinary cell call across town.

"I'll come back," he said. "I'll come tonight, stand by."

But no, not yet. Linnie and Ro agreed on that.

Linnie was so proud of Cam, the first member of the family to attend graduate school, the first person to win prestigious notice of any kind.

Ro shared the pride, of course, but more than that, she worried. A gift like Cam's had to be fragile. He would feel Greg's every needle prick, every unbearable ache. He would empathize fully and doing so would damage him.

Much better for her to take his place, for her to be the one comforting Greg through chemo, bringing him cooling ices, playing music for him. She imagined herself a heroic figure, inspirational in her devotion, admired by everyone.

She didn't understand until later how pathetic it had been to regard Greg's struggle through the prism of her fantasy, rather than as its own miserable self. For misery it was, and real, and she turned out to have no stomach at all for that. Not that she didn't try. For months, she went wherever he was—hospital or house—every day. Well, every day at first. And then the days became like drops in an IV infusion, causing pain in a rhythm of hoped for cure and certain suffering.

As the weeks passed her tasks contracted to two. She played the piano every evening while Linnie and Greg sang hymns, for as long as he had breath for it. And she kept the brothers talking.

Four Skype calls every week didn't sound like much, but the time differential alone could be tricky. Greg's best period was late morning when he would have energy, and look as healthy as he ever would. But eleven a.m. in Texas was five p.m. in England, and that opened the black hole subject of Cam's evenings without Ro. He'd pledged faithfulness with persuasive intensity, but a whole year in such a place? How could a person of Cam's temperament fail to fall in love at least once?

The longer he was there, the more certain she became that it had happened, was happening. A conversation on Skype is off center, because of where the camera is located. When he talked to her, Cam usually focused on the screen where her face appeared, which made it look like he was talking to her left breast. About three months before he came home, that changed. He made sure to look right into the hard, round glass eye of the webcam when he told her how much he missed her.

2011

Ro is obsessing. She can't get the idea of the church organ out of her head. It makes no sense, musically. She hasn't played an organ since she was twelve years old, at her grandmother's house—one of the homey kind suitable for sing-alongs. She tries to imagine what the instrument in the old lady's church would be like. Certainly not a grand baroque job, with towering gilded pipes. Something smaller, something she would be able to handle.

She misses playing, it's true. Her professor called her crazy for coming to the country like this without a piano, or arrangements for using one. She had to, though. She had to clear away the clutter that kept her from seeing clearly, from noticing. She had to give no nourishment whatsoever to the insistent demands of abstraction, the pleasures of imagination that distract you from what is really going on.

All week she struggles with herself.

She's curious, okay? She's a tourist here, and wouldn't a tourist want to see a local object of interest? Famous, the old lady had called the organ. How many famous things can there be in such a small town? She and Cam have hardly gone anywhere since they arrived. Nowhere just for fun, to explore the local sights. She hasn't really wanted to drive very much, given the ugliness of the drouth-scarred landscape.

On Tuesday, though, she has an opportunity. While Cam visits the bank, Ro uses the truck. It doesn't take long to find the church—a wooden building, painted white, on a bluff that overlooks the Coyote Creek watershed. Below her, pastures you would expect to be lush in early summer have faded into the thin grays and browns of grass bitten to the very root.

Hot dust on the driveway lifts around her ankles in futile gasps as she walks to the church door. Rain would settle it, but the locals say it hasn't rained—really rained— for more than three years. In a drouth of this duration, the occasional sprinkle hardly counts.

The church is country Gothic with windows of frosted glass and a wooden double door. But a stout rod has been wedged between the pavement and the twin door knobs, barring entry. She stares at it, stupidly. Tears, welling up, are the last thing she expects and she rubs at them with her fingertips. She gives the rubber base of the rod a little nudge of annoyance with her toe, and is surprised when the shaft topples into her hand. The door falls open.

The air inside the nave is still, sun struck. It's an unpretentious interior of white walls, simple wooden pews, and a painted primitive altarpiece of Christ, wrapped in a red cloak, borne into heaven by three angels.

The organ in the loft overhead is scarcely bigger than the arm-span of a large man. From below, she can see the hand-turned cedar pipes that produce the sound, and the shining gold-painted screens in the shape of wings that are its only decoration.

The stairs are right there, in front of her. Should she go up? The diffidence that Ro has internalized from childhood, the fear of treading on the sensitivities of other people grips her now. She hesitates, but they are only a few stairsteps of painted wood. She'd like a closer look.

In the loft it seems harmless to sit for a moment on the organist's bench and run her fingers over the keys, so familiar in their simple configuration. Before she can play, however, someone will need to operate the bellows, a small box-like contraption attached at the side. She should have thought of that. Such arrangements are common for an instrument of this age. It's unreasonable for her to feel so thwarted.

A strange thing happens after her visit to the town. Ro stops cleaning and, instead, she begins to read. She had been a reader from her earliest years, even before music. Oh, yes. She had read a page out of The Hobbit when she was barely four. Her mother had been sitting at her dressing table, lining her eyes with thick black pencil prior to going somewhere, and she'd not believed Ro was really doing it, until she looked at the page herself. True, they had a CD of the book that Ro had listened to about a thousand times. But the day she started to read, the disk wasn't playing. She had just picked up the book and out came the right words.

Theirs was a house full of books with secrets and information in them that reading unlocked. At all hours, Fran would find Ro sitting cross-legged behind a chair, or sprawled on a sofa with one or another unsuitable volume. Art books with paintings of naked people in them, stories by John Updike. She couldn't possibly understand what she was reading, her father said.

One day when she was five, Ro asked, "What is a cunt, Mommy?" That night Fran and Tom took down all the remotely racy books and sealed them into boxes that Ro found years later in the garage, half consumed by roaches and silverfish.

The replacements were child-appropriate works about horses, dogs, adventuresome little girls of one kind or another, usually detectives or orphans. Sometimes both. Encyclopedia Brown, although male, was a favorite.

Maybe her parents thought piano was a way to "pry her nose out of a book," which was how Fran put it when talking to Tom. Ro isn't sure. But she took to music immediately, as she didn't with drama or ballet.

From then on, Ro remembers a constant struggle. There were the demands to be and do what others expect in the daily world of school and chores and family. Against those clamored the internal requirement, equally strong, to remain in her own head, to follow the path that her imagination led her along through stories or through music. A need to escape reality, in other words, has been what drives her.

If her mother were here now, she would tell Ro that the little organ was a sign, especially the fact that it couldn't be played without someone to help, to work the bellows. That was even more significant than the mysterious way she'd learned of its existence. Because Cam could help her, of course. All she would have to do is ask.

Reading, however, she can do alone and here.

Instead of going off to use a piano, or organ, she can stay in the house with Cam where the only sounds are the refrigerator's hum (middle C), and the air conditioner's whine (G sharp). She can read and he can work, and the machines can spin and turn as they would do anyway, without conviction, as though the house were holding its breath.

*

Fucking meds. He hates the way they flatten everything, turn him into a fingering chimp batting at the keyboard, making only dead words in lines that look like mere strips of font face, black on white emptiness. Not sentences. You could almost lift the lines off, wrap them around your finger or fold them into little accordions of irrelevance.

But he doesn't stop typing. What else is he going to do?

He's quit the meds before and slowly the words come back, for a time, not very long in actual count of days, but a relief all the same. Then Ro catches something in him, he never knows what, and back he goes to the facility. Incarceration. No more, no less, no matter how Dr. Full-of-Shit cocks an eyebrow at the term. Prisons don't need walls, your head is a prison, your skull is a prison.

He wants out. Out, away, up, blue sky words, Greg's forgiveness, his own forgiveness. Ro. Confession is good but he can't. The way he feels is a palimpsest of what's needed. Too much has been erased. The person who betrayed Ro and Greg barely exists any more.

And Ro is always here, always hovering. He knows she thinks she loves him, loves some image she has of him, no longer accurate. She loves his family, the scab that meeting him allowed to form over her own losses, but that's been torn away, now, by Greg's death and his own attempts to follow.

Theirs has become the kind of connection that binds long married couples, fused by shared calamity and blurry guilt. Before Greg's illness, they had planned a wedding when Cam returned from England. They would move to wherever he found a job. He would write and they would teach and she would perform whenever the opportunity arose. They would build a life.

What they're doing now, instead, is more like a panicky patching of the roof between storms, making sure plenty of buckets and pots are placed to contain the leaks. Her warmth, her passion for music that was so much like his for poetry, has burned down to a concentrated nub of determination that he will not relapse. He feels it like a brand.

III.

2011

"Crap," Cam says from the bathroom, early one July morning.

"What is it?" Ro is in bed, floating in the backwash of a dream. She'd been swimming underwater. As the drouth drags on, she thinks about water all the time, longing for it, endless bodies of water shimmering and cool.

"I've run out of meds."

"Oh, Cam." Can this possibly be true? She knows he counts them carefully. She raises up on an elbow. He is standing by the sink, squinting into the mirror.

"No problem." He runs a testing hand along his jaw.

But it is a problem. The pharmacy in Bernheim is at least an hour's drive away, going and coming back. Ro dreads these longer highway expeditions—the blare of crisping fields, the stunned distress of trees. Riding in the truck with Cam, she feels the drouth climb in with them, press down on her until breathing, itself, becomes an act of will.

"I think I'd like to try it alone today," he says in the same thoughtful voice. "I'm doing a lot better."

True enough. And a solitary venture might be good for him. It would prove that someday this degree of reliance upon her will pass.

As the dust settles behind Cam's departing truck, Ro feels a guilty rush of release. Do something for yourself is what they tell caregivers, isn't it? It's what she has become. Nevertheless, the idea smells of indulgence, like playing a Chopin Nocturne just for the pleasure of it. Or Bach, even on an organ. For a moment she allows herself to think how it might sound, the voice of that little instrument in the church that speaks to a yearning for beauty, for transcendence, among hardscrabble lives.

She walks up to the road, but it's way too hot for a run. By the mailbox she notices the remains of a snake, now only a dark squiggle of decay against the road's ashy surface. Stunted grapevines and spindly cedar saplings line the fence, and she sees no animals at all—not even a turkey vulture circling over the fields.

Under the bell jar of the drouth, the land is weirdly quiet. It feels false, the wrong side of a glass through which she can see faint images of the life she might be living, where Greg worries about the SAT, and where her parents fuss over their first grandchild, where she and Cam are married and she has not yet learned the shallow nature of her character.

2009

In the late middle of Greg's ordeal, when she, herself, had begun to flinch at every needle, she'd received an invitation. A chamber music festival in the countryside outside Houston—not far from where she and Cam are now, in fact. They needed a pianist to substitute for the one who'd cancelled and her professor had recommended her. The festival was highly thought of, attended by people from the city, as well as the local community. She'd been so grateful for the change of scene—for two days and two nights away from illness, sorrow, her own inadequacy in the face of such suffering.

The principal violinist at the festival was Japanese, a visiting fellow at the University that year. Naoki.

Naoki had been a revelation, his playing so clear, so supple, so perfectly attuned to the other members of the ensemble. The grace of his bowing hypnotized her, the command in his hands, small but finely boned and strong. He smelled of something new, not sandalwood exactly, not resin. When they played together, her piano and his violin, the music stitched them closer than she'd ever been with anyone. Through it, she could express her despair over Greg, over her own inability to handle it, and never feel the need to confine the pain with words.

The weeks afterward—the trips back and forth to Austin until Naoki left—became for her the unacknowledged shadow on the time of Greg's dying. Naoki was the excuse she made to herself for not doing more at the end. For not doing all she should have. For not doing what Cam expected of her and what she expected of herself.

2011

Inside the house while Cam is gone to Bernheim, Ro imagines his empty, cell-like study, the powdery neglect that surely defaces all the books, strewn papers, open notebooks filled with his scrawl. She knows how he works, how the distribution of clutter mirrors the intensity of his focus.

It's unhealthy for him to spend so much time each day in a place like that. She knows ways to remove the dust around his disarray without disturbing things. While he's gone, she can slip in and clean it so carefully he'll never know she's been there. He hasn't asked her in so many words not to, after all. It seems a kindness, a gift, when thought of in this way, an opportunity for her to make up for letting the house go lately. She gathers up her materials, the rags, the dusting spray, the electrostatic duster on a stick.

But there's no need for any of them, because there are no books or papers or notebooks in the room. No dust. The table he uses for a desk is pristine and empty except for his closed laptop. Her heart begins to pulse in her throat. She is going to open it. Her hand shakes with the realization that this has been her intent all along.

Throughout their time together in the country she has never snooped on Cam, not his writing, not his email. It has been a point of pride with her, that she would not pry. He will tell her anything important when he wants or needs to. They will tell each other. She has believed in this openness, this transparency, despite every action of theirs that clearly demonstrates the opposite.

She awakens the computer's display. Without a password, his files are all right there for anyone to see. It doesn't take long to find the one he's currently working on. A substantial file.

Has he ever written prose of any length before? His fellowship was for the terse poems he built around desperate, inexplicable acts, so that the reader felt the humanity of the perpetrator. When asked, he said he trolled the internet for subject matter.

This is very different.

Nnnnnnnn, it begins, just n's in a line, a whole page of n's. Then more pages, more nnnnnnnnnnnnnnnnnn nnnnnnnnnnnnnnn nnnnnnnnnnnnnnnnnnnnnnnnnnnn

nnnnnnnnnnnnnnnnnnnnn. After a while, they become NNNNNNNNNNNNNNNNN NNNNNNNNNNN NNNNNNNNNNNNNNNNNNNNNNNNNNNN.

Her face goes hot and she keeps scrolling. Is this an experiment? Is it going somewhere?

O's appear. Then t's. A word is spelling itself out. N-o-t. Not a good sign, even when h follows and she's paging down quickly now because it all adds up to NOTHING. Pages of the word, broken into component parts, remixed, and, at last, gathered into the shape of one letter per page, a giant N comprised itself of N's, a hulking O, and so on. One hundred and ninety-three pages, so far.

Even at her most constricted, even when she couldn't hear the music her hands played against the rushing noise of panic in her ears, it was never, ever, nothing.

"Hey," he says, half-smiling as he comes into the kitchen. "Cam?"

He edges a look toward her, a little slip of a look.

"I opened your computer."

He stops in front of the fridge. His face is half turned toward her, an eyebrow raised. It's like he's waiting for something.

And now she understands. He'd done it on purpose, gone off and left his file unprotected for her to find.

"You see," he says in a curiously satisfied tone, "I'm fucked. It's all fucked."

Never in tune with the thin harmonies of contemporary life, Ro has been unfashionably worshipful of Cam, of his brilliance, the heights and depths to which he could take her, just by talking. His poems had shone for her with the same gleam as the perfectly struck notes of Horowitz, a kind of mental foreplay with guaranteed results. She never allowed herself to wonder what it would mean if he lost his ability, if he went mute, so to speak. If he became ordinary.

For the next week, Ro can hardly keep from following him around. The property they're renting has outbuildings, a metal barn and shed. There are plenty of sharp tools, rope, poisons.

She finds herself assessing his every move, every sigh. On the positive side, his expression shows no sign of a downward drag. Her mother had adopted the classical face of tragedy after her father's death. Ro thought it was like a Mardi Gras mask that she'd take off when the season was past. Cam doesn't seem to be wearing any kind of mask, but she can't imagine who he'll be without the writing.

"I'm going for a drive," Cam says on Saturday, much too early. His tone is casual, although there's nothing casual about the break in routine.

Ro straightens from loading the dishwasher. "Let me get my stuff," she says.

"You don't have to come." He has his keys in his left hand and is flicking them with his thumb. No backpack.

"You don't want me to?"

"I've got some things to think about." He moves a step closer and the absence of the touch she anticipates feels disturbingly intimate. "I appreciate all you've done, Ro, but it's not right for you to sit here every day with me. You've let me interfere with your life."

Ro tries to breathe normally. After all, it is daylight. Maybe he just wants to get away for an hour or two.

"We've changed, Ro. We haven't wanted to face it, but the people we were before don't exist anymore."

Ro's mind scurries through a series of possibilities, each one triggering its own different tone of buzzing alarm. "Do you know how long you'll be gone?"

He works his jaw and shakes his head. He won't look her in the eye.

A practical thought occurs to her. She has no car. She hasn't needed one. "Cam," she says slowly, "if you're away for any length of time, you know I'm stuck here. Did you think of that?"

A flicker of irritation passes over his face. She is conscious of the keys in his fist and the tension in his arms and shoulders. She thinks of the deer they often see in the fields. Poised. Ready to bolt. Just as likely to jump in front of your truck as race away.

"Maybe you could at least give me a lift to town?"

Ro isn't sure what she expected would happen after Cam drove off. It was one of those occasions where she simply followed where her feet led, one foot coming after the other quickly enough to prevent her from falling face forward onto the pavement.

No one, not even the women moving about the altar, saw her climb the stairs. If Cam were there, he would have admired the little handmade organ, the care and patience of its maker—working without a blueprint, the sign said, just the memory of the organs he had known in Germany.

She should have noticed that first day that the bellows contraption, in its anonymous, unadorned box, speaks to a different, more functional, spirit. The box is machine made, just like a motor housing. And, yes, there is a switch, a perfectly obvious small lever switch she hadn't noticed before.

Reaching for it now, she doesn't consider the women below and the fact that she is there without permission. She simply flips the lever and the bellows fills with a wheeze. The keys are pleasantly springy under her fingers, and the familiar notes of the Bach G-Minor fugue come into the church through the old cedar pipes like breath.

The voice she summons belongs to a boy on the edge of puberty, pure and high with the slight hoarseness of tone that signals how quickly the voice itself will be gone.

Widow's Brain

There, beside a bin of green bananas, Agnes O'Toole. No mistaking the woman's substantial bulk, her small head on its long neck. Odd, how much Agnes resembles a goose of the folk-art variety, especially in that billowing white skirt. Now Agnes cranes her neck and swivels her gray head (gooselike!), as though she hasn't the slightest idea what's next on her list. Or, more likely, she's looking for Bob.

Bob.

Marion's heart gives a delayed *thud-dump*, and she ducks into the snack food section. She slips on reading glasses and pretends to care about the arcane additives in items she doesn't use. It will be all right if neither O'Toole develops a yen for Doritos or processed bean dip.

She emerges to see the white skirt sashaying alone out the exit behind a double handful of green canvas bags—identical to the ones Ted bought and Marion never remembers to bring.

When the checker sees Marion, the woman's face rearranges itself sympathetically. "We were so sorry to hear about Mr. Osborne."

"Thank you, Verna." Everyone is so careful. It's as though Marion would notice her bereavement only when it's mentioned. Beyond thanking them, though, what can she say? What does she feel, for that matter? She fumbles at the catch on her purse. "I didn't know the O'Tooles lived around here."

Verna keys in the code for the frozen dinners. "Word is they bought at the old Lionberger place. The people are selling it off in ten acre lots."

Marion knows the land. Before the drouth it was a lovely terrain of rolling pasture interspersed with stands of cedar, a few gorgeous spreading live oaks.

"I guess it was bound to happen," she says and lays two twenties on the counter.

Going home, Marion makes a short detour in the direction of Lion's Head Acres, as the signs call it. "A goddamned subdivision, girl."

She's talking to Katie, the dog in the back seat, but it's not Katie who's listening. It's Marion, herself, needing to fill the silence. Except it isn't wholly silent, is it? Not with Ted's voice yammering away inside her. Right now, he's giving his familiar rant opposing the breakup of large farms, the arrival of second homes like theirs on smaller tracts. Oblivious to irony, was Ted. *Think of those extra toilets, those dishwashers and washing machines.*

He'd been against their own yard sprinklers, too, certain even that modest use would draw down the aquifer. *Without the aquifer, none of us will be living here. You wait.*

He had reason to worry. The long dry period had des-
iccated the region, toppling trees, leaving others—cedars,
post oaks—as gray reprimands among the surviving stands
of summer green.

Off to her left, at the top of a hill, the ancient live oak
canopies of La Bahia cemetery are thinning like an old
woman's hair. Marion finds nothing peaceful about rural
graveyards. What she hears beneath the serenity is the
relentless transformation underground of what was known
and loved. Or feared.

Ted wanted his ashes scattered on their property, but
he never said where. Maybe that's one reason why, right
now, the cremains—hideous word—are sitting on a book-
shelf at the house, beside *The Geology of Petroleum in
Texas.*

If their daughter lived nearby instead of in Brooklyn,
Ted would have been sprinkled over something weeks
ago. Evie's idea of the event comes from sentimental
movies where two or three sad people fling a cupful of fine
powder off the edge of a pier. Nothing mentioned about
the accompanying fingertip-size chunks of disturbing
bone. There was bone in the ashes of their dog, at least.
Was it different with a person?

"I'm coming next weekend, Mother. We're going to
get it done. I'll book a car in Austin." That was Evie,
yesterday, checking in from somewhere out of doors.
No mistaking the windy background noise, the traffic.
She usually phones Marion in between meetings, either
walking fast or in a taxi. Marion can always hear the hurry
in her voice.

"I have to go, now," Evie said. "See you next Saturday."

"Darling, the urn is in Houston—," Marion began, but the line had gone dead.

Evie doesn't understand. The last time she came, the pond was clear and full. Now Marion would be slinging remnants of Ted into a slick of mud and slime. Or scattering them across a field of cracked gray earth among jewel-backed beetles and stinging fire ants. Marion can't bring herself to do it. Whatever she feels about him—disappointment, annoyance, spite—something prevents the final step.

A rumbling noise, loud and urgent, rises behind her—a gravel truck closing fast on the narrow dirt road. She pulls over as far as she can, and still she cringes. These county roads were meant for slow-moving farm machines, tractors, balers, that kind of thing.

By the time the dust dissipates, Marion's only wish is to get home as quickly as possible. Why should she care where Agnes and Bob O'Toole live? What are they to her anymore?

"Have you been up here long this time?" Didi asks, when Marion finally sits down. In from Houston for the day, her old friend has already settled herself on a spindly wire chair. Husband Geoff has disappeared in the direction of the barn to check out Ted's shop equipment. Marion will let him take what he wants.

"Only a few weeks," Marion says. "I was nervous about coming alone." If she doesn't come, though, rot will set in. The unwelcome heart-shaped vine whose name she can't remember will infiltrate the eaves, detach the molding. She'll have to sell, unless she can handle the place on her own.

They sip from sweaty glasses of Prosecco. It's hot on the porch. Rivulets of condensation from the ice bucket make a wet circle on the tablecloth. Didi's short colorless hair has frizzed into a diadem of wisps. Fine hair, post chemo.

There are no nibbles to go with the wine. Marion feels a flutter of alarm. "Did I offer you cheese and crackers?" The moments of situating herself and Didi on the porch have erased themselves.

"You did offer and I declined in favor of lunch." Didi—who's still far too thin—lowers her voice. "Don't worry, dear. It's the fog of trauma. They call it 'widow's brain.' It should wear off."

The term, vaguely repelling, carries the echo of "chemo brain," but Didi's memory has improved after eighteen months. She no longer gropes for as many familiar names and words. Marion feels a twinge of guilt for equating Ted's expected loss with her friend's health disaster. Besides, Marion's own deficit is more like what a hurricane survivor might feel—as though important belongings have been swept away. Stabilizing ones she didn't reach for every day but knew were there—pictures of her parents, Evie, Ted as a young man, serious but sweet. She lays her palm against the bucket's chilly steel exterior. "You'll never guess who's moved out here—Agnes O'Toole."

"Poor Agnes," Didi says. Her tone brims with unspoken information.

"Why *poor* Agnes?" A shiver of expectancy.

Didi looks down at her glass. Unlike Marion, she's still part of the old group, privy to its news.

"Tell me." Marion leans forward.

"Awfully sad," Didi says, pursing her lips. "Bob made some bad financial decisions and they had to sell the house on Del Monte. He's in an Alzheimer's facility, now, not far from here."

"How terrible." Strong-jawed, good-looking Bob, blank-eyed. The what-ifs that cling to a person are all fumes.

"You know nothing serious ever happened between us." Marion needs to emphasize that. The way Agnes had turned on her had been the small scandal of their bridge circle.

"I know, dear," Didi says and pats her hand.

After lunch Geoff drives them to the shops in town. At Marion's suggestion, they follow the scenic route past Lion's Head Acres. "If you want to see where Agnes is living, I think it's the next gate." She keeps her tone casual. Her curiosity feels almost prurient, certainly unkind. She has dreamed of payback, though, that's true.

Didi leans forward for a better look. "Geoff, turn here."

The odor of recently spread asphalt seeps into the van. On both sides of the drive, the land looks stripped and raw. Singleton live oaks share patchy fields dotted with piles of rust brown brush.

"I don't know which one is hers," Marion says, although no houses have appeared yet.

"There's sure a lot of water in the lake," Geoff says, nodding to his right. "Remember that party when old Ted nearly clocked the guy for keeping his stock tank pumped full just for show?"

Marion does. A hollow space opens inside her.

"Here you go," Geoff says, slowing. Behind a white picket fence, two small kit homes form the ell of a single cottage painted the color of milky coffee. Rustic limestone surrounds raised flower beds, the kind Marion always wanted, but Ted refused to pay for. The mailbox confirms O'Toole.

"Very nice," Didi says. "You'd almost never know it was pre-fab."

"Her vegetable garden probably has tomatoes already." Marion imagines the woman's long-necked, wide-hipped figure in overalls with a picturesque straw hat, bending over a row of well irrigated beans. Agnes would be sure to handle any calamity so much better than Marion can.

The next morning, Marion goes out early to inspect her own garden. Each crunchy step through parched grass propels an arc of grasshoppers.

Ted appreciated the garden's daily surprises, good and bad. He did all the work himself, and when, because of the drouth he decided to stop wasting water on grass and flowers, he never stinted on his tomatoes, squash and melons.

She would have let the plot go this year but she didn't like the thought of Ted frowning at her indolence. By now, though, he'd be scoffing at her eight tomato plants, one neat row of herbs—basil, prolific oregano, some thyme.

If everything withers in the drouth, she and the yard man will simply turn it under. Maybe add Ted's ashes to the mix, a disposition he might actually appreciate. Marion can't do that, though. Evie wouldn't allow it. She'd be sure to sense her mother's ambivalence.

A flicker of black and white near the neighbor's fence. Marion stares. Please not a skunk. Katie, nosing around in the monkey grass for rabbits, lifts her head.

The low branches of the yaupon thicket separate, and a border collie trots toward them. Its coat is matted with grass burrs and dusted with the awful white clay the county uses to stabilize their road, but she can hear the jingle of tags. Someone's lost pet, then.

When the two animals have smelled one another long enough through the yard fence, she lures Katie back into the house with a piece of breakfast bacon. Minus the attraction of canine company, the visitor will surely go home.

An hour later, though, the dog is still there, panting in the shade.

Marion fills a bucket from a hose and opens the gate. She hears Katie's muffled whine from the mud room window, the scrabbling of claws on the glass. When the collie stops drinking, it wags up, sweet-faced, and allows Marion to pat its grubby head. She fingers one of the metal disks that dangle from its leather collar. *Finn* is the dog's name.

Maybe she's been expecting it, in the way what's on your mind can manifest in what materializes around you, but *O'Toole* on the back of the tag doesn't come as an actual surprise. Newcomers can be clueless about the dangers a pet encounters running free in the country: mother cows, mean ranch dogs. The inevitable gravel truck or pick-up. Whether the collie got out by accident or intent doesn't matter, though. He has to be returned.

Marion sinks onto the garage sale bench where Ted used to rest in the middle of his chores.

She hasn't spoken to Agnes in how many years?

It was the late eighties, near the middle of their respective marriages. Sort of like the middle of a Texas summer, when the red pulse of discontent sets in.

Agnes had chosen to marry a casual flirt, that was her fundamental mistake. And Marion's? Marion had married a man with imagination only for the workings of machine systems, geological processes, for the ebb and flow of subsurface hydrocarbons.

Until the day she found the note in a pocket of the green golf sweater Ted wore at work, she had believed he was faithful. She still doesn't know if there were other affairs. She had never confronted him. In her family of thin-lipped West Texas Presbyterians, no one ever challenged anyone directly. If they had, who knows what discomforts might spew forth? And anyway, the details scarcely mattered. She was already too angry for anyone's good.

Along about then, she'd noticed Bob O'Toole, the way a face in a crowd suddenly becomes someone you recognize. She'd seen him before at parties, the handsomest man in any room—and maybe he had attempted to flirt with her, she can't remember. This time, however, she was primed. But what had it amounted to, really? A couple of lunches, a drink in a bar, one fumbling—and wholly unsatisfactory—encounter in his office that still makes her wince in embarrassment. The intensity of her attraction, though—her need—had been shocking.

Whatever it was between them ended in the hallway of his house during the third hour of the O'Tooles' annual holiday buffet. Right where Agnes could see them. Saw them. Stared at them. Bob's hands gripping Marion's bare upper arms, her palms pressing against the lapels of his navy cashmere blazer. Pushing him away, surely.

And what if Agnes hadn't seen them? Would Marion have let it go further? Met him at a sleazy hotel with a bed that squeaked? Met him again? Heat prickles her neck and face. She had seen him once, hurrying to meet her, a hunched, furtive figure, the very opposite of anyone's dream man. Shame had propelled her away from the window then and it rises, still, after all this time, entwined with dusty traces of desire. For a moment, she had thrown off the morality of her upbringing. She had looked into Bob's hazel eyes across a couple of martinis and seen herself as someone far more alluring than Ted realized, and certainly more appealing than Agnes.

That night at the party, while Agnes watched, Marion had walked away from Bob vaguely pinked with satisfaction, as though she'd won a primitive contest no one admitted was going on.

But she hadn't won anything, had she? Because afterwards, Agnes extracted Marion from the life of their group as efficiently as a chef removes a smelly gland from a leg of lamb. No more invitations. No bridge tournaments, no trips to the beach for boozy days and nights of cards and laughter. Through a combination of charm and ruthlessness, Agnes wielded social power, the only kind available to Southern women of their generation. Marion felt certain that if Agnes were forty now, instead of seventy, she'd be CEO of a large corporation, or the general of an army, a position from which she could ruin many lives instead of only one.

A few of Marion's friends had remained in touch. Didi, one or two others.

Soon thereafter, Ted bought her the house in the country and Bonnie, the first of their Labrador retrievers. Like Katie and the pets who came between, Bonnie was a rescue dog—rescuing Marion, that is, from constant reminders of what her stupid indiscretion had cost.

In front of the O'Toole picket fence, she opens the hatchback. Fastens Katie's nylon lead to Finn's collar and gathers herself. No way to prepare, though, for what Agnes will say. Together, she and the dog move quickly up the walkway of smoothly mortared stone.

Finn dances at the end of the leash. His tail pops against Marion's calves.

The door opens.

"Oh!" It's more a breath than a word and Agnes drops to her knees in the way Marion no longer can. She plunges her face into the collie's thick, bedraggled fur. For a moment, there is no sound except a muffled weeping, not the sort of thing an adversary, if that's what Marion is, should be witnessing.

Marion retreats a step, and imagines Bob in the hallway of the nursing home, one of the wheelchair-bound array of slack, thoughtless faces, shrunken shoulders, knobby hands. Gone from our shared world as certainly as Ted.

Agnes wipes at her damp, dirt-streaked face. "Thank you, thank you, so much." She looks up, then, and recognizing Marion, frowns. "Where did you find him?"

"He turned up in my pasture this morning," Marion says.

Gripping the porch rail, Agnes pushes to her feet. "I heard you had a place around here," she says, in a cool tone. "I saw Ted's notice. I'm sorry for your loss."

Etiquette doing its lonely, necessary job.

In the prickly silence they bend forward simultaneously to unclip the leash and Marion gets a whiff of sour coffee and unflossed teeth. An old woman's smell.

Both of them. Old. So damn old.

A knot of ancient grievance loosens, just a little. Why on earth should any of it matter, now? One widow and one as good as, neither of them any longer the people they once were.

"I'm glad Finn found me, Agnes," she says. "I'm glad I could help."

On her way home, Marion thinks again about that note in Ted's pocket. A scrap of yellow paper, not so much folded as scrunched. Blue ink. Ted never used blue ink unless he was signing a legal document.

This Wednesday? was all it said, two words in Agnes's handwriting. Marion knew the script well from invitations and thank-you notes over the years. But had she thought of Agnes the first time she saw it? Or had that been later, after the nonsense began with Bob?

She tries to remember the sequence of events surrounding the note. Inserting her hand into the pocket of his sweater, her fingers closing on the crumpled paper. The next thing would have been to smooth it out, see if it was a number Ted might need, or a list, perhaps. Did she do that? She can see how it might have been, the paper curling on a table, her hand—the meaty side of her palm—pressing it flat.

Infidelity had been her first thought, that much is sure, although he might have been given the note without responding. It could have been related to work in some way. She had never let herself consider alternatives for more than a second or two. She had been so sure betrayal was what it conveyed.

The hurt and anger she felt, then, were real, just as real as the longing she had for his infidelity to be true. Only its truth could justify her behavior with Bob and the guilt she would feel afterward.

That foolishness ate at her, still, the humiliation of being attracted to a man everyone else knew slept around. Ted had been so stifling in those days. Questioning her casual opinions, pointing out errors of logic. Marion became almost afraid to comment about anything unrelated to domestic arrangements—the house, meals, social engagements. "Your sphere," he called it. He made her feel trivial. No wonder she'd bloomed at the first sign of male admiration.

Ted couldn't help it, though. His drive to be precise, fill in every blank, complete the cycle of a thing, was inborn. He might have had no idea how desperate she became under the glare of his searching, critical eye.

Oh, why must sex be so complicated? People love their husbands. Surely the easiest, simplest thing is to love the person you spend your life with.

Instead, she'd tended her anger as carefully as Ted did his garden, nourishing it, periodically, with her silence. Whenever she saw him laughing or talking seriously with another woman, at dinner or cocktails in a group of new friends, Marion would find herself sliding away.

"We've hit the mute button, I see," Ted would say, when she stopped speaking, but two or three days of the silent treatment, and he wore down. The tender area below his eyes went thin and papery and she knew she'd won that round. This was before he got sick, of course.

She had made herself believe that a withdrawal of that kind was the best way to punish him, when what she'd really been needing was to punish herself.

Needing it still, in fact. Only a severe punishment could rid her of the terrible fear, growing in her now, that she might have hurt a decent man without any cause, and kept on hurting him. That she might be the kind of person who would do such a thing.

A Wall of Bright
Dead Feathers

1.

In front of the stone farmhouse, Lavis hesitates. She should go inside. Face the eyes that will swing toward her and squint in a hunger for knowing. Years have passed, but they're still her family—siblings, cousins, the Old Man himself. They will catalogue everything—her simple dress and jacket, her unassuming flats, the evidence of time in her face. They will find her wanting. She pivots off the walkway into the irrigated grass. The stepping stones are right where she remembered.

Past the arc of unnaturally green lawn, the fields fan out, so dry they seem more nearly gray than brown, the color of aged kindling. The pasture should have been grazed down by now, but the Longhorns are gone—moved, or sold off. On the day she left, the steers nearest the fence had raised their heads and watched as she drove by. She remembers their spotted hides, cream and red, their improbable, impractical horns.

At the rear of the house the steel and glass expanse of

the addition her father built when Lavis was five glares out over the lake below. Beyond it, hay fields unfold to the crest of a distant hill.

Thirty-odd years ago, she had a screaming row with him over the ground water he pumped to keep the lake scenic. She had opposed the waste. She had opposed many things he wanted—particularly his disappearances during her mother's illness and his remarriage so soon after she died. He got his way, of course, with wives and water. He usually did. The best she could do to retaliate was leave.

People indoors crowd against the glass wall of the trophy room. Relatives, she supposes, migrate from one hug and handshake to another. In their pressed jeans or prairie skirts and ostrich boots, they look costumed. Lavis thinks of presentation gift baskets done up in gleaming cellophane.

What, really, is she doing here? The creamy engraved card read: "T.D. Caldwell requests your presence for the celebration of his 90th birthday." With it a note in an unfamiliar handwriting: "The company interests will be disposed of. Your presence is required."

That part especially made no sense since she'd been disowned twenty-five years ago—twenty-six, now—but she had come. She had felt compelled to travel somewhere following the departure of her most recent ex. Who had elicited actions from her so extreme they shame her now beyond any thought of groveling before her father.

The Dickist, as she thinks of the man, *post facto*, had proved unreliable in ways that involved a younger woman, mannequin-slim, draped over and around his unfaithful body in photographs it cost Lavis far too much to acquire. She had been reduced to that.

And much worse. It was as though another person had lived inside her all these years, and only now stepped out to take over.

While he was at work, she had let herself into his place with her key, pulled out his favorite sweaters, the DVD's they'd watched together, all his monogrammed shirts. He kept his restored '65 Corvette in a shed behind the house, secured from the elements under a dust wrap. She removed the wrap, stuffed the gear in the front seat, saturated everything with charcoal starter before settling the duster over it again as lightly as a mohair throw. Several sloshes of the flammable liquid to weight it down, followed by a lighted match and it was done. At the corner she called 911. Even from the freeway she could hear the sirens of the fire department.

Two hours later, exultant and horrified, she was in the air, on her way from Atlanta to Austin.

A door opens in the wall of windows and a man comes out. He wears an unzipped fly fisherman's vest with many well-stuffed pockets. His faded jeans are unbelted. In her experience, men wearing jeans without a belt drink too much. She detects no odor of alcohol, but there is something...

"I don't like crowd scenes," he says, moving by her on crepe-soled shoes. He leans against the deck's railing and gazes thoughtfully at the lake with its one extravagant shimmering willow.

"It's because I don't like to listen," the man says.

"I'm Lavis," she says.

He turns slowly. "Pierre." Bi-tone eyes, one gold-flecked green, one pedestrian brown, blink at her out of his sun-starved face.

"Pete?" Her favorite cousin—it has to be.

He smiles.

"Have you seen him yet?" No need to specify. The only *he, him* that matters is her father.

"Not yet," says Pete.

"I wonder if he is, you know, intact."

They're silent for a moment because ninety is not really as old as it once seemed, not with all the octo- and nona-genarians toddling about on prosthetic knees and hips, running slow marathons, jumping out of airplanes.

"Do you think they'll feed us soon?" she asks. "I missed breakfast."

"Lunch is at noon. Did you have any trouble coming from Austin? If you came by 71, you must have seen the wildfire."

"What fire?" A momentary flicker of confusion, resolving.

"They've been fighting a blaze near Bastrop for the past week, a big one. Perfect conditions for it, I hear—heat, wind, dry grass. We're under a burn ban."

2.

Caldwell began that morning a little after four a.m. with a cup of low-acid coffee that he made himself in the study adjacent to his bedroom. He drank it in a rocker by the screen door, feeling the stir of soft air, so different from the processed air everyone lived in now.

As far as he could tell without his hearing aids the house was quiet. That's how he liked it—quiet, with help nearby. He'd felt increasingly fragile since his last scare. Bladder cancer, the result of forty years' worth of cigarettes and cigars, the surgeon said. It hadn't yet come back. Maybe it wouldn't. A stroke was his greater fear, being unable to move or speak. He'd spent his life controlling others. The idea of being controlled terrified him.

And today felt like foreshadowing. He had always directed family votes. Or they had directed themselves, because the decisions—mostly confirming the size of a payout—were easy. This would be different. Not only was the scale of the distribution much larger—they'd like that—but the implications were greater. For one thing, it would be the last payday. After this deal was consummated—if it was—the company would cease to exist.

Why should that trouble him? He should be viewing it as a business matter, like so many others. Instead, he kept seeing the small county roads around this ranch. They were barely two lanes without shoulders, and empty most days unless you came upon a farm vehicle carrying a lone bale of hay. The machine-formed bales were round, and often wider than the tractor.

Driving those roads over the past sixty-odd years, he'd grown accustomed to long stretches of pasture on both sides, broken only by the occasional barn and scattering of cattle. He liked to see the peacefully ruminating cows lying in the shade of live oaks on a summer morning. The flutter of wind-stirred grasses along the verge seemed beautiful to him.

So much of that would be lost if what was planned came to fruition. He understood the effect better than most people did. Caldwell Energy had been in the Eagle Ford shale from the beginning. He had watched as Dewitt County roads in south Texas crumbled under the assault of tank trucks, dump trucks, equipment trucks more numerous and far heavier than any the farm-to-market roads were designed to carry. From an office in Houston's hazy sky he authorized the laying down of well pads, several acres wide, and the drilling of horizontal wells every few hundred feet in some areas.

Patriotism—the push for energy independence—demanded it, he thought. Money, too, of course, so much money that before long patriotism lost out to the siren call of export.

He had not allowed himself to care about the consequences of disruption—how it affected the ranchers who might not have kept their mineral rights, who would be bearing all the upheaval, the dirt and noise and worry about water, the smells and just plain ugliness, without any balancing compensation. When a well was fracked, you could feel the trembling miles away.

There, at the beginning, he'd been the company's strongest voice pushing to drill when drilling—and finding—seemed a salvation more sure than any religion's promise. He'd been right, too, about the finding, anyway, and now a new set of shareholders would be clamoring, as impervious to argument as any zealot. They will see his ambivalence as a sign of weakness.

3.

Lavis edges into the trophy room and presses her spine against the glass wall. She lifts her chin to survey the other occupants, none of whom have noticed her.

What does she expect to happen, today? What does she want to happen? Her disgust for the life of her upbringing has not diminished. Every good material thing that came to her before she left had its origins in damage to the earth, above and below ground. The truth of this situation had never registered, not once during all those years of growing up, until her father's arrogant waste of water drew her complacency aside.

As for the stuffed carcasses surrounding her now—ibex, elk, and moose, two grizzlies, a trio of exotic big cats, one in full, glorious pounce—only in the heat of her great illumination had she sensed at last the odor of death. Powdery, with a slightly sour note. Maturing taxidermy.

Perhaps it was the giraffe that tipped her awake. Just days before she left, her father had workmen mount the animal's head and neck that still protrude from the middle of the long wall. Part of the neck, that is, enough to make clear what the animal had been. Visualizing what wasn't there made her understand for the first time the ghastly change he'd wrought on the creatures who stared at her with their shiny glass or acrylic eyes.

She marvels at the consistent nature of the Old Man's taste for animal remnants. The present collection of at least four hundred small stuffed birds had consisted of about fifteen when she left, clustered over a doorway. Today, it's an entire end wall, a crazy quilt of bright dead feathers.

A man approaches Lavis with two mimosas in hand and a white-toothed smile.

"I hoped you would come, Lavis. I'm Jake Taylor, company attorney."

A Saturnine presence with his pale skin and straight black eyebrow shelf. That smile would be used only for purpose.

She accepts the glass. "Where is he?"

"He'll make his appearance in about five minutes, I've been told."

An unwelcome swoop of adrenaline. "How is he?"

"Still sharp, if that's what you mean," says the lawyer.

Across the room several people turn and stare in her direction. Lavis ducks sideways. Taylor moves into her line of vision. He isn't large, but he's wide.

"So it's like that?" he asks, more sympathetically than she would have expected.

"I don't recognize them." It's much colder in the room than she realized.

He turns slightly. "Left to right, Marjie Beckhorn, husband Tad, and Azelee Ames. Your—"

"—half-sisters." Her glance catches his, and part of a giggle shakes loose. "They never used to be *that* much younger. I suppose I've still got a brother?"

Taylor nods, dropping his smile. "Walter has Parkinson's," he says. "He's with the old man."

At that, the door at the near end of the room opens.

Her father, moving slowly, remains an erect presence, thinner than she remembers. He wears flat-heeled boots, a khaki western shirt with pearl buttons. His hair, dark and blow-dried, has silver tips, like the chinchilla coat he'd once bought for her mother. The stress lines on his jaw follow the same gravity-defying tilt common to the women in the room. Human versions of the shooting trophies, stretched smooth and sleek over a relentless structure.

Behind him shuffles a bent figure, leaning on a cane— Walter, in a plaid sports jacket and Cordovan loafers. Her long-jawed big brother.

Taylor whispers, "I'd down that drink now. Last chance."

She complies. She'll want a seat somewhere unobtrusive.

"You're on his left side, just there."

Oh, God. "Why?"

The lawyer shrugs. "Orders. Walter's on his right, at the head of the table."

The single long table runs beneath the giraffe. It's set with silverware, glasses, and ranch water in pitchers engraved with her father's interlocking TDC.

"What's going to happen? Why am I here?"

"Can't say."

Lavis, aware of a growing weakness in her legs, makes her way forward.

The Old Man, already seated, ignores her approach. A little translucent wire snakes out of his visible ear. Someone places a cup of coffee before him, and he nods.

Her brother hooks his cane on the back of the chair beside the O.M. and sits. He doesn't acknowledge her either. She spots a small microphone clipped to his lapel.

"Good morning everyone," he says, in an amplified voice. "I'll be chairing this meeting, at T.D.'s request. I'd like to begin by welcoming a new attendee today, my sister Lavis."

The beam of his unexpected notice leaves a sensation of scorch. Walter had never understood her reasons for leaving.

Lavis is detaching the last stubborn morsel of barbecued chicken from a drumstick when she hears a gunshot. Her stomach clenches.

"Our neighbor has a shooting range out back of his trailer," Walter says.

The O.M. is patiently chewing, not looking at either of them.

Another report. Not a shotgun, she decides, although her experience with firearms ended a long time ago. "He sounds awfully close."

"He's a veteran, so he knows what he's doing. I'd prefer he'd chosen another time for it."

Walter's words are followed by a fusillade—twenty or thirty rapid shots. A hot, brittle sound.

Lavis resists the urge to stand up.

Walter frowns. "Must be a special occasion." He lifts a trembling forkful of charro beans, half of which fall off.

A momentary sadness tugs at her. Walter had been such a graceful boy.

"Seriously," she says. "How far away is that shooting range?"

"You're in Texas, Lavis. Bear that in mind."

Slices of birthday cake and ice cream are being distributed when a hatless man in desert camouflage arrives on the deck. Knocks three times on the glass door.

Lavis can see no weapon.

Jake Taylor hurries from a side table to greet the visitor. The young man—very young, she notes—ducks his blond head and murmurs something.

The O.M. begins to eat.

Taylor comes over to Walter. "He says he's sorry to disturb the party, but his well is sucking sand. He seems agitated."

Caldwell raises his head with his lips parted so that the contents of his mouth are visible. Lavis looks away.

"And this has what to do with us?" asks Walter.

"He says it's the lake that's at fault."

The O.M. grips Walter's forearm, whispers in his ear.

"Take our visitor into the library," Walter says.

For the first time, the O.M. glances at Lavis. He cannot be pleased to see her smug smile. It's what she always told him would happen, pumping water for a decorative indulgence.

Everyone is eating cake and drinking coffee when Walter and the O.M. return. No sign of the young man.

Walter raps on his glass. "We're sorry for the interruption, folks. While we enjoy our dessert, we'll have this presentation of our company's history, a tribute to the vision of our founder."

One or two people start to clap. Shades crawl down over the windows, while the wall of birds divides and slides away to reveal a large screen.

4.

While the film plays—Walter's idea—Caldwell mulls the unsatisfactory conversation that just took place with Bo Carter. His young neighbor isn't aware that it was Caldwell who sold him, considerably below value, the land he lives on.

Caldwell did it for the boy's mother, a lover from his Paleolithic past who had remained a friend. Bo's war experience had turned him inward. All he wanted, now, was peace, his mother said. Best for him to be alone somewhere, best for him to work with his hands.

Too bad the kid had dug a shallow well. He hadn't done his homework. Sucking sand for a few days was a good way for him to learn a better decision-making process.

Anyway, on Monday Walter will get a deep well put in.

Up on the screen the narrator is pointing out various parts of a shale rig. The scraped surface around the well of tightly packed, trucked-in light gray sand looks like patches of desert.

Caldwell can see it as a critic would, the stripping away of vegetation, the flattening of earth to accommodate the large pads required for deep horizontal drilling, the construction of eight-acre ponds for supply.

Detractors follow their suppositions down the hole, into the possibility of broken casing that would allow chemicals to infiltrate ground water. They jump to thoughts of pipeline explosions and spillage, of oily residue on doomed seabirds, miles away from the production site.

They don't think about the light switch or the central air, the grocery store two miles down the road they'd be walking to in 95 degree heat, or higher, if they had no gasoline. They don't think about the store's refrigerated cases of ice cream, milk, eggs, butter. Beer. They don't understand that their entire lives, even their clothing—petrochemical-based textiles like nylon, spandex, polyester—must be considered, weighed, against a few drowned birds.

Caldwell accepts that man has influenced global climate change but he apportions the bulk of responsibility to the demand side—to the people of his country and the world who want what they want, right now and cheap.

He can't foresee any solution. People don't like to make transformative changes in their lives. They don't like to look ahead. Because if they do peer into the diminishing tunnel of the future, what they will see most clearly is the impassable wall of their own death at the end. The workaround offered by religion's frantic embrace just provides an even greater certainty that nothing will be done to prevent the planet's ruin.

Ruin already underway in Africa. He was so fortunate to have been there during the time of the great herds, when the eco-structure that supported them was still mostly intact. His family doesn't understand that the trophies staring down on them even now in the darkened room are a monument to that lost world. A labor of love, no less.

The opponents of mounted animals see only the dead part, the creatures stopped in their prime. They don't think about how short that prime is, how soon the beauty of these beasts reduces to bone.

He remembers the giraffe's loping grace, his own sharp regret when the nephew of an associate—first time on safari—brought her down without warning or approval. Caldwell certainly wasn't going to let the beautiful creature lie there afterward for hyenas to tear apart. By now, of course, every other member of that giraffe's herd is dust. True for contemporaries of the ibex, too, the great elk, the various breeds of deer, even the birds. Only these examples remain to embody the glory of one animal's particular life.

Against such magnificence, he had felt small, insignificant in his human awkwardness and the limitations of his body.

5.

In the fifteen minute break that follows, business trappings replace the evidence of a meal. Notepads, pencils arrive at each place alongside forest green folders festooned with the Caldwell Energy logo.

Halfway down the table, Pete leans forward with his head in his hands like he is dozing. Why aren't they all asleep, after so much food and the interminable presentation?

Her father isn't drowsy, though. His eyes sweep the room like a raptor's.

Lavis opens her folder. On top, the agenda. The main task involves ratifying the acts of the board over the past year, so maybe the shareholders don't need to be sharp. Under new business, the words *Grand Destin* give the only indication of anything unusual. A resort hotel?

The O.M.'s expressionless face inclines toward the paper in front of him. Even the thin, bony hands are still. She sits back in her chair. She'll be able to leave before long. It was ridiculous for her to come. Did she expect her father to embrace her, show forgiveness, show any feeling? Is that what she had wanted?

And what will happen when she does leave? In all likelihood, the police are looking for her. The Dickist will surely file charges. He loved that car.

She is such a fool.

The words "new business" bring her attention back to the meeting.

"We have some very good news today," Walter is saying. "We have an offer on the table to buy Caldwell Energy for the generous sum you will find written on page three of the proposal in your folder."

Nobody's asleep now. Papers rustle as the shareholders scurry to page three.

"We can have discussion," Walter says, "but first I would like to move that we empower our board to accept the offer of Grand Destin Partners. You have the written motion attached to your agenda, along with a paper ballot. It requires a second."

"Walter, if I may?" Caldwell's voice is not strong and his face is pink with the effort to project. "I'd like a word before parliamentary procedure complicates things."

Walter unclips the microphone and hands it to his father.

Lavis pages through the documents. Destin's brochure has been printed on thick, glossy paper reeking of chemicals. At the back of the folder, she finds a letter, like an afterthought.

Her father is giving her two hundred shares of company stock. For a moment she can't catch a breath, then she's flicking through the proposal, looking for the per share value.

There. She sags a little in her chair. Just two shares would save her, pay for the lawyer she'll need, make generous restitution. Two *hundred* shares is almost lottery money. It will change her life.

"I can't say that I expect you'll vote to turn this down," Caldwell is saying. He stops for a moment and reaches for water with his free hand. Does he notice Lavis has seen the gift?

He replaces his glass. "You ought to know, however, what your vote means for this place where some of you spent summers growing up.

"It's no accident that we haven't worked deep around here. I've made sure we avoided the mess—busted roads, dust, noise, odors—and the water draw necessary to the fracking process. Water is a significant cost, considering the drouth we've been suffering through.

"When these Destin boys take control, we'll get the whole ball of wax. They'll pump the water they need. Truck in what they can't pump. And when it's used they'll dispose of what they can't afford to recycle. Usually it goes somewhere for deep injection.

"Most of you don't live here, or near here, but I do, and I would greatly prefer not to inflict this on our neighbors. We're in a scenic area, where many of the homes are second homes, and the owners don't have more than a stamp's worth of mineral rights, if that. We're destroying their investment, and their happiness, for at least a generation. And why?

"All of us here have plenty of money—most of us at any rate. I used to think that more was better, but now it's looking to me like the hardest part of business is to know when you've got enough. I've got enough and I'm going to vote my shares against this motion. They're not quite a majority, as of today. The rest of you are on your own."

He hands the mike back to his son and slumps a little in his seat. A waiter appears at his elbow to refill his water glass.

"Thank you, Father," says Walter. "We still need a second."

"I'll second," says Azelee, in a breathy, careful voice. Three years behind Lavis, her half-sister had been a cheerleader, known for her sexy post-game hoarseness.

Pete raises his hand. "Is it certain they'll drill around here?"

Walter looks over at his father.

The O.M. nods. "I would if I were them. The geology works well enough."

Walter's left hand flutters like the wing of a hungry nestling. He thrusts it into his jacket pocket. "Is there more discussion? If not, we'll move to a vote."

Lavis scowls at the ballot. She gets it, now. These shares are more than a simple gift. They're part of the argument.

What he has said today changes nothing. He embodies a lifetime of assault upon the land. All of her relatives are manacled to the ease and privilege they have enjoyed. They will fight to the death of everything they love to assure comfort continues for as long as they themselves are alive.

Lavis has always tried to hold herself apart. Even now, she's the only one in the room dithering, it seems.

Walter scrawls something, hands it to her. *There's been no dilution. Your shares come out of Father's holding. Your vote will tip the balance today.*

She picks up her water glass, slippery with condensation, and drinks. Her father is only pretending to cede control. He assumes she'll vote against environmental damage and reject the offer. Abstaining means a stand-off.

If she votes for it, though, and lets the deal pass, she will be free, really free. She can buy off her ex. He'll be able to own ten Corvettes. She can travel, live anywhere, surrounded by beauty.

Her heart opens at the prospect. It's like arriving at last in a high, clear place where breath comes easily.

But it's not a neutral choice, is it? The act of voting

means accepting the shares. She would become as complicit as anyone in the choices he has made with his life. The only way the Old Man doesn't win their argument is for her to reject the stock outright. What will happen then—will the stock revert to him?

Everyone is watching her, avian eyes, beaks, a predatory flock.

Her father's eyes rise to her face, briefly, and drop again.

Or she might have this all wrong. He might simply love her.

A uniformed security person she hasn't seen before comes up to Walter, murmurs something.

She hears the sound of a distant siren.

And now she smells smoke. More than barbecue, less than the barn next door, as the old saying has it. A few people crane necks to look outside.

"What's going on, Walter?" Pete asks from his end of the table.

"We've been informed there's a small grassfire nearby, but we'll be fine."

Beside her, the Old Man begins the laborious process of getting up. He's using a cane with a handle carved in the shape of a heron's head.

Through the glass wall, over the deck, the lake, the sere hayfield spurts flame randomly, like droppings. She'd always imagined an approaching wildfire as a solid wall, not these almost insignificant flares…quickly connecting. In the time it takes to inhale, half the field is alight.

"Walter…," she says.

Pete is half out of his chair. Azelee's husband pushes back from the table. Walter lurches to his feet. His own cane hits the floor with a resounding thwack.

The O.M. reaches the door that leads out onto the deck.

"Activate it," he says, clearly, audibly, to the security man, standing there.

A panel retracts, revealing a large touchpad. The officer taps in a code and almost immediately generous arcs of water spew over the house and yard, sheeting the glass, obscuring the view. They hear the growl of a heavy pump in the vicinity of the lake.

Sirens are coming closer.

Her relatives cluster against the window, trying to see through the curtain of water. Some are hugging each other.

Lavis tries to imagine how it would feel to burn alive, and isn't surprised when her mind refuses to comply. The spray will protect the house and yard for as long as there is water in the lake, in the aquifer sands below. For as long as there is electricity or gas to pump it.

How predictable. The imminent hazard, the expectation of reprieve, the Old Man's confidence that technology will provide it. Every one of them today joins him in this complicated faith, that, here at the end of his life, or near it, they can continue to rely on her father's ingenuity, on the power she has always struggled against.

When the danger is past, and the shareholders—her only family, after all—are slouched in various stunned postures around the room, Walter reminds Lavis that the vote is not complete. She hears this while riding limply in the backwash from adrenaline, gripped by a weakness that she has always believed comprised her truest self. She can barely lift her arm.

Later she will decide that she was driven by thoughts of the good she could do with so much money.

She will continue to think of this every evening in her exorbitantly priced condo, sipping a gold-struck Russian River chardonnay while seated in the vintage Eames chair she has positioned for the best view over San Francisco Bay—even now cooling into the purest of cerulean blues through lightly tinted floor-to-ceiling windows.

Silences

Alys appears on the front porch at a little after seven. A soft fog clings to low places in the field between her and the caliche road. She can't see the road, but she'll hear it when the pickups begin to carom past on the way to work, wheels squirting gravel at the bottom of the hill.

For the moment, though, all is a purity of silence. Not even the birds are singing. With the sack of seed under her arm, she steps into the damp grass.

In the beginning, the absence of the city's constant mechanical growl bothered her. Didn't people always say that in the country, whispering? It's so quiet. What was that weird noise?

But normally, it isn't quiet at all, not with the hum and chortle of birds during all but the hottest hours of the day. And especially after dark, when there's no bustle of human activity to obscure the fusion of night voices, frogs, crickets, the almost feline purr of a screech owl. She has learned to find the moments when the chorus stills, vaguely ominous, suggestive of a creature passing whose presence puts every chirping, chirring organism on alert.

Alys fills each feeder to its brim. She likes the look of generosity—an extravagance, Dale tells her, and it's true, since raccoons come along in the night and strip whatever's left. She enjoys imagining the birds' pleasure, though, to find

such amplitude in a place where previously there had been only rough dallisgrass and the everlasting briars. She smiles as she makes her way back to the house and breathes in the last moments of quiet. Soon Eric will be up, ignoring her pleas to eat breakfast.

Dale? Well, Dale is somewhere, the barn probably. He will expect strawberries, out of season, for his cereal. She sliced them last night, sprinkled them with sugar, noticing as the juices began to ooze how each slice resembled sections of a tiny, bleeding heart.

Later that morning she heads to town for supplies, the daily chore. They usually need something—milk or snacks, if nothing else—but the main objective is conversation. Ritualized conversation, the kind that can make shopping such a comforting experience. The proprietor will ask her by name if they've had any rain out at their place. Alys will say no, not yet, but tomorrow looks better. And she will inquire whether the toddler granddaughter scurrying among the vegetable bins is feeling better after her cold last week. Connection. Connection unburdened by too much actual knowledge.

At the deli counter, waiting for her usual order—Black Forest ham, Havarti cheese, pitted green olives—Alys startles at a sudden eruption of laughter. It's the coffee drinkers, a group of men gathered in front of a display carousel containing nails and screws. The store keeps a pot going there all day, with powdered creamer and paper-slip sweeteners and what look like little cocktail straws, for stirring.

She can pick out Dale's resonant voice. She doesn't pretend to understand how this rural community operates. Maybe telling jokes is how you sell garden and construction tools. Dale has never sold anything before that you could hold in your hands, certainly not hardware, but he has learned a lot about renovation over the past couple of months and they need the income.

In truth, she's relieved to have him away from the house for part of the day. The place is much too small for the competing egos of her son and husband. Dale has always been so sweet to her. It's difficult to admit, even to herself, how sick she is of his constant need to appear self-confidant when what's underneath is as soft and squishy as the insides of the black beetle she stepped on ten minutes ago, getting out of the car.

Always he must be right and Eric wrong, no matter the subject, until the tension in the house becomes as unavoidable as the smell of a mouse decaying in the walls. Not now, though. Now, Eric's back in school, a sophomore whose brains should put him at the top of the class even though he appears to have acquired an allergy to homework. At least, she never sees him doing any.

Alys, smiling thanks, reaches up to collect her food, neatly packaged in white paper. The town is a paragon of order, grass clipped, streets bare of trash. By dawn the day after the summer festival, the grounds of the square where people ate funnel cake and cotton candy and drank syrupy grape drinks or beer, looked as pristine as if no one had walked there in weeks. It's the German heritage, Dale told her, a matter of pride in taking care of things—a trait he clearly admires.

She consults her list. What's next? Dairy. Paper towels. Bananas, if they're not overripe.

The day before, Eric brought home his first friend at this new school. The boy was quiet, nice-looking and polite, and they spent a couple of hours fussing with the old four-wheeler Eric had unearthed in the barn, beneath a spidery tarp.

As a boy, Dale flipped that very machine on the bank of the pond—the stock tank, Dale calls it—after which his father forbade him to ride it. The vehicle had been sitting, forgotten, for more than thirty years. You can use it, he told Eric, if you can get it running again.

A potentially dangerous project of his own, just what a boy needs.

*

Full moon. Brighter than Eric likes. He'll have to be careful. He knows the sightlines from his parents' bedroom in every direction. The woods cluster around the yard in a semi-circle. Lots of cover. His heartbeat is the loudest thing he hears as he slides open his window, steps out onto the sloping metal roof of the porch. Sometimes he just sits out here and smokes weed, shines a flashlight into the field behind the house, hoping for a wolf, maybe, to be pierced motionless by the light. Or, a bear would be great. Does this fucking nowhere even have animals like that? Or anything worth seeing? He knows there are feral hogs. He's heard his dad curse them for the deep furrows they make rooting under the trees. If he could get his hands on a gun, he'd kill one. He'd squeeze the trigger slowly, watch the hog plop over. Like Grand Theft Auto, but soundless. Oh, except for the gun going off. He has never heard or seen a real gun fired.

He grabs the rope he's fastened to the bed's frame and lets himself down the roof slope on his belly until his feet find the porch rail. He drops easily from there onto the soft soil of the flower bed his mom's been working on. He scuffs over his footprints so it looks like an animal was digging. Bo, maybe, except Bo doesn't dig. He wishes Bo could come with him, but the dog sleeps in the parents' room. Too risky.

In six seconds, he reaches the stand of cedar and hard-woods that lines both banks of the creek and he can turn on his flashlight. He knows there are snakes but he doesn't worry. He asked for snake boots for his birthday and got them, even though most of the snaky grasses had been cleared. He plods along in them now, secure up to his knees, feet cushioned in thick, comfortable socks.

He has discovered that he can hike along the creek for several miles in each direction. There is almost no water on account of the drought and when there is, one bank or the other provides enough open space for passage. The woods amaze him, fallen trees or living straight trunks draped with spider webs that give way suddenly into moonlit glades. In Houston, he'd never seen a forest, except for parts of Memorial Park, and his mom would never let him go there alone.

He keeps expecting something astonishing to appear, in the center of a clearing, maybe, silvery gray in the moonlight—a big buck, or wolf or a mountain lion, even. There've been cougar sightings nearby, and he can hear the coyotes howling in the night.

He pictures what he would do if one of them, fangs dripping with saliva, suddenly launched itself at him from behind a tree, like the trolls do in Oblivion...He drops into a crouch as he moves and it seems that the shadows take on the contours of the monsters that populate that game, congregating now in the darkness around him. Even though he knows he's pretending, his heart beats faster. His muscles tense. His hand finds his knife—a boy in the country should have a knife, his dad told his mom—a machete would be better, though, a long, sharp blade. He'll try for that at the store. His dad is so fucking ashamed that he'll get him almost anything he wants, as long as Mom isn't around. Dickhead.

*

Saturday morning, the week before Halloween. At the sound of the 4-wheeler, Alys looks up in time to see Eric disappearing down the gravel track with Scott, his friend, perched behind. He's gone most of the time now, the black clothes from Houston replaced with a vintage version of urban cool, white t-shirt, sleeves rolled up; black high tops, low slung jeans with no belt, retro hair slicked back. A peer group of two, he and Scott. She wonders what the other kids think. Eric used to care about that.

His room has become disconcertingly neat as well, like no one lives there. "You don't need to clean it, Mom. I've got it."

Who expects a fifteen-year-old to act so responsibly? She should be grateful, but instead her skin tingles with alarm. He should be messy, mercurial, even angry in the brooding way he has been ever since they came here. No, he shouldn't. Is she insane? She loves the calm, the peace of his absence.

Her happiest moments, in fact, come when both of them are elsewhere. Dale and Eric—the people she loves best in the world, her world, shrunken now to the circumference of their demands. The feeling is not acceptable, she knows. Only a shallow person would feel that way.

In truth, however, she'd rather be where she is right now, on her knees by the porch, wrist deep in the lovingly amended, rich-smelling soil as she sets out the pansies and dianthus she hopes will brighten the coming bleak winter.

It's the social season in Houston, at least one charity event each night if you've a mind to take it on. Does she miss that? Not really. She misses the challenge of working on them, though, the committee politics, the trouble-shooting. Dale used to say that her job was surprisingly similar to his, although she could hear the condescension in his words. Well, he was right about the relative significance. It wasn't her work that ruined their lives when things went wrong, was it?

Her fingers probe the earth around the hole she's dug,

loosening its perimeter so the roots can penetrate easily. She rarely wears gloves to garden. Her nails will crack, but she doesn't care. Who's going to see them? Besides, she likes the way the soil feels, the smell of fertility and hope that surrounds her as she slips the small plant into its place, presses the earth down around it, moves on to the next.

Eric's midterm grades were disastrous. In Houston, he'd always received A's and B's; now they lodge among the lower C's, with a D in Spanish, of all things. The boy's hurting, however he shrugs off her efforts to help. Grades aren't her bailiwick, though. It's Dale's job to hand out praise or correction. Besides, Eric doesn't listen to her. He can be looking right at her and he won't hear a word.

The evening they got the report, Dale sat there in his chair staring at it while his face darkened and the veins in his neck stood out. Her shoulders tensed in expectation that he would come leaping up, bellowing for his son who, flouting the usual ritual, wasn't even in the room. The occasion required a swift, clear father's response. Instead, Dale had done nothing. Just sat and stared at the card until the blood retreated from his face. The reality is he has no stroke. He left his authority in Houston, alongside the life he demolished.

She rocks back on her haunches, for the moment oblivious to the beauty around her, deaf to the whispers of dicky-birds, to the notes of a cardinal's repeating call.

The slanting amber light of fall is sad. That's all. It makes her sad.

*

The word comes just after four in the afternoon while Dale is washing his hands and thinking about that first delicious gulp of cold beer. The hearing in the civil case is set for the following week. He will have to appear in person, and the attorneys want to go over a couple of things beforehand. A couple of things. No biggie, that's meant to convey, but the actuality can be as encompassing as sky.

He doesn't tell Alys right away. Dinners are bad enough lately without a load of useless speculation, every piece of it scudding across the surface of his dishonor.

He pours a second beer and sits at the kitchen table, where they take their meals. The kitchen is no bigger than the pantry of the house in Houston where they lived until last spring. He has complicated feelings about the physical aspect of the change. Familiarity is part of it. His parents had done well, but that hadn't seemed to require the supersizing that his own peers consider basic. This room feels right to him. Its height, width seem natural. He had admired the high ceilings and openness of the rooms in Houston, but the truth is, he always felt a bit unmoored, like he might find himself some night bouncing untethered against the ceiling.

The downscaling, too, seems—is—appropriate.

He believes he has allowed no one to see the full scope of his desperation. Any sign of confusion or uncertainty, and the fragile triangle of his small family will fragment. He's sure of this disintegration at the same time as part of him denies the possibility as too dramatic. He opposes drama in all forms.

In silence at the old fashioned stove, Alys is giving the pot of vegetable soup a final stir before ladling it out into bowls, which she will set on the table beside plates of cheese and bread. Eric drifts in. No one says a word.

When they begin the meal, she retreats to the porch with a glass of wine. Usually she'll eat with them, at least, but the net is the same. She won't say a word to him until they're in bed. Sex? Forget it. Twice since they got here, each time after she was fluidly pliable with drink and they coupled furtively in the reddish dark behind his eyelids. He couldn't bear to see her eyes. He passes his hand across his forehead and reaches for his wine.

Eric, across from him, keeps his head down, slurping up soup in the noisy way Alys always corrects. Dale starts to say something, but the words die in his throat. When Eric pulls the whole half gallon of chocolate ice cream out of the freezer and heads for the stairs, Dale just looks away. Who is he to tell anyone what to do?

*

Two o'clock in the morning and Eric's heart is racing. He's been looking forward to tonight for weeks. They're going to flashlight some deer. Illegal as hell, but so what? Deer season is about to open and when that happens Scott says you never see the fuckers. You should go before. Right before. Tonight. Scott is getting his grandfather's gun.

"How?" Eric asked.

"Dude, he sleeps like a fucking dead man. Not a problem."

Scott isn't like Eric's friends back in Houston. He wouldn't fit in with any of the groups. Not jock, not goth, not nerd. One of the things Eric likes about Scott is he's unpredictable, not like these other guys who can't talk about anything but beer and sex. They don't have a football team. Not even six-man. How do you get that? Eric misses football. He likes to hit. He likes to feel his shoulder take a guy in the ribs, drive him down into the grass. He doesn't even mind the pain. Lacrosse, too. Motherfuckers here never heard of lacrosse. He stumbles. His boot catches on a root. Shit. He didn't expect it to be so dark. Without a moon, it's a lot harder than usual to move along the creek. He's probably spooking every deer for ten miles.

Scott gets irritable when he has to wait. Eric doesn't like irritable when it's aimed in his direction. But he doesn't have far to go by the waterway, longer by the road. Man, the creek is so fucking perfect. They can dig in on a mud flat inside the nature preserve that owns the land, and any buck or hog or fucking unicorn for that matter will be dinner. Skin it, section it. Scott says his dad taught him how before he split. Scott lives with his grandparents, both of them so Deutsch you expect *sieg heil* instead of hello. Not fair, he catches himself. Scott's Oma is really nice, she makes great cookies and she's not stingy with them either. She fixes these giant sloppy sandwiches when they go off on a Saturday, too, on black bread with thick cheese and sausage and homemade sweet pickle relish. "Have your-selves some fun, boys," she tells them on the way out.

He told Scott once that he thought he was lucky to have a grandmother like that. Scott went silent for a moment and then he spat on the ground, a honking oyster. "I'm like you, bro. Stuck here. Nobody fucking asked me, did they?"

Eric checks the glowing dial on his watch. 2:17. Perfect. He's seen tracks along the creek, down the woodland trails. Deer wear a path, just like people do. The prints of their hooves show their weight, their size, how fast they're moving. This creek is a fucking deer interstate, you think there'd be a coyote at least behind every tree, just waiting for sweet hot bleeding meat to wander past. Not that fucking vegetarian shit his mom dished out for dinner tonight. How does she expect him and his dad to stand it? Not that his dad would say anything.

*

Dale turns over and looks at the clock. Two-thirty. Alys is sleeping the sleep of the pure of heart, on her back, mouth open, breathing softly. He walks over to a window and opens it. The air is cool and sweet, not cold, and Saturday is Halloween. What will they do? Their first Halloween here and he doesn't have clue one what the local customs are. Alys will know if there's something at the school. They should all go, in costume. Dressed like the people they used to be. Hah. He'd wear his white spread-collar, striped custom shirt, pin-striped suit. Alys can wear her Jimmy Choo's and that black silk dress with the green pashmina that matches her eyes. Eric can wear his old football jersey.

The taste in Dale's mouth is freshly sour. It's a dark night and completely silent except for Alys's untroubled breathing. How have we come to this? He asks himself for the one-thousandth time. How did it happen?

But as he stands by the open window with the breeze riffling the hairs on his chest, the answer that comes to him is different from what he usually hears. It's saying that it doesn't matter. That this isn't so bad, really, when you think of what might have happened. That this is, in fact, enough, and he will be satisfied with it, if only they don't throw his ass in jail next week. If only they give him time, the rest of his life, to pay them back. The thought goes out from him into the night and he realizes then with mild surprise that he's praying.

*

Scott's not sitting on the log at the mud flat when Eric gets there and, at first, Eric is pleased. He shines his light around the log and gives it a kick in case of scorpions, then plops down and pulls out some weed. He's a little nervous. He's never shot a gun and he wishes he'd had some practice. He's heard that shotguns kick pretty hard. They're not good for deer, either, he read, not even with buckshot in them. A rifle is better. But Scott's grandfather has a shotgun, a ten-gauge, and that's the only option.

He draws in a lungful of smoke, holds it. He kind of likes weed for the way it smooths things out. He'd had some back in Houston, but not like regular or anything. Scott, two years older, has other stuff, too, and hints at the crazy goodness of it—like walking on the moon, he says—but Eric is resisting. Eric still wants to play sports—if he can find a fucking sport in this dump. Track, maybe, in the spring. Track might be good.

He hears some rustling in the underbrush and half turns to greet his friend, but nothing's there. No human thing, anyway. He looks for the telltale flash of green retina, the height will tell him what it is, but he sees nothing and the sound doesn't repeat. He takes a big hit of weed, sucks it way down.

*

Alys tools along in the truck, with the windows open and the air lifting the hair at the sides of her face so she feels a trilling of youth. A beautiful morning. She won't let the image of Eric's dark circles at breakfast get her down. She swears she smelled marijuana on his clothes when she popped them in the wash, but she's never seen any sign before. Has she been missing something? He didn't so much as grunt before he shuffled off to catch the bus, shoulders hunched like he was expecting punishment for something he'd done. She dismisses the direction this thought leads, and concentrates on the yellow and gold and russet in the trees that arch over the road. It's positively weird how her spirits levitate these days just about as abruptly as they droop. Maybe she's going into the change. Oh, Christ. Not yet. Please.

She pulls up next to the ice machine at the store, the only empty spot in the parking lot. Dale's not working this morning. Instead, he's back at the place, fixing fence. He wants hamburgers for lunch, so she'll check out the meat. The store got its delivery yesterday. A perk of the rural lifestyle, you know when the bread comes in, the vegetables, the milk, the cookies she sneaks in the afternoons.

Two women, wider than she is, crowd the aisle, murmuring, and they don't even look at her as she slides past them, heading toward the meat case. Their faces have that puckered look you see when somebody has died. A local dignitary, she thinks. There are a lot of retirees in the area, and people are always dying. The funeral notice will be sitting on the counter by the cash register, right next to the packaged brownies and mini-pecan pies. You have to be careful not to set your sweaty milk carton on it.

She is surprised to find whole wheat buns on the bottom shelf of the bakery section. They inspire her. She'll cook the burgers on the charcoal grill, serve them thick and rare. Now if only there's a tomato ripe enough to have some taste.

The checkout counter is deserted when she sets her basket on it. Donelle and another woman whose name Alys doesn't know are making sandwiches a few feet away, preparing for the noonday rush.

"You hear about the Schmidts this morning?" Donelle says, coming toward the register, wiping her hands. The woman's normally cheerful face is somber as she picks up the first package.

Alys, still tasting the possibilities of a better than average lunch, half smiles. How many hundred Schmidts would there be in this area? "No, I didn't. What happened?"

Donelle runs the buns through the scanner, picks up the onions and puts them on the scale. "They got killed. Right there in the house last night, not far from you."

Alys's hand freezes halfway into her purse. She knows those people.

"They got the boy who did it, too," Donelle is saying. "The Schmidts' grandson. That Scott boy. Haven't I seen your son in here with him, the two of them together?"

Alys can't find the breath to speak, at first. "My God. What happened? I mean—"

"Shotgun. The boy admitted it right out to the police."

"But...but why? Why would he do that?"

Donelle shrugs, drops the last onion into a plastic sack and knots the handles so they form a loop. "You want this on your ticket?"

A Skeptical Parrot

I. Central Texas, 1862

1.

Conrad doesn't rise from the table with scraping chair and sudden gesture, but he does leave. He will not stay to be insulted.

Outside, he sucks in chill, cedar-scented air. Every discussion, now, spirals into acrimony. Always the subject is slavery, the war.

The dirt road that splits the village winds past a grove of leafless post oaks that extend their skeletal tracery into an overcast sky.

His stride is rapid and his feet strike the packed earth with force. His friends, for they are his friends, do not understand.

A man must have his work.

Moments later, rounding a curve, he comes upon a young woman, lost in thought, standing in a freshly swept yard. She is holding a broom while the soft light pours over her still face. *Deutsch* light, here in this foreign place where refuge had seemed possible. He does not speak. Speaking would break the perfection of the scene. Gray sky, dark shape, pearlescent skin.

Although Conrad rarely draws the human form, he yearns to begin, and fears beginning for how the very process would alter the image he longs to hold fast. A forbidden image, for he recognizes her as Johanna, whom his friend Leopold intends to marry.

2.

Johanna drags the heavy chair behind the barn so it can't be seen from the house. Can't be noticed by her cousin, Ursula, who disapproves of endeavor unrelated to chores.

The rest of Johanna's meagre equipment is already in place. Sturdy board, pens, ink, paper of a suitable weave. She clips her half finished drawing to the board and opens her specimen book. *Sabatia campestris* is her subject, dry and flat as iron and time can make it.

Shortly, the Texas Star will scatter its bloom across the meadows. She remembers from last year the living hues—the deeply stained magenta petals that surround a vivid yellow outcropping of stamen and pistils. Although the colors have dimmed, it scarcely matters, since she works in black and white. She'd prefer color, but she has no pigments, no funds to purchase them, no knowledge here, on the frontier, of the source from which they might be purchased.

Some of these impediments would melt away if she married Leopold. For three months, his proposal has shouldered itself into her household routines like a large piece of displaced furniture. A *shrank*, perhaps.

She should give him an answer, but what, precisely, would she say? Her present duties allow moments for botanical study, for plucking and pressing the wildflowers, making her intricately detailed drawings. Such necessary occupation, difficult enough even now to manage, will not survive the birth of children, the care of her own household. It will not survive marriage itself.

Behind her, a shuffle of boots on the rough ground. A man coughs politely. "You are wise to press them," he says.

It's the painter, Conrad, Leopold's friend.

"Don't stop, please. I am interested in what you are doing."

She feels a pleasant surprise, tinged with embarrassment. No one pauses to watch her work. No one pays attention to the growing number of sketches that she carries to the locked wooden box beneath her bed.

He considers her drawing with a gaze that is serious, evaluating. "The outsize scale provides an arresting dislocation—to think of this tiny flower as if it were larger than a peony," he says.

The bounteous peony, which cannot grow in the harsh Texas climate, had been her Oma's favorite. Even as a child in Germany, Johanna had felt its creamy froth of petals catch at her throat. Demanding something from her for which she had no words.

"We rarely notice a single wildflower," she says. "It seems unfair."

He studies the fine line, the tapering of a petal's edge. "The original displays a striking pink. You will add this?"

She does not answer. The truth would invite pity.

He hunkers now beside her chair. "I might be able to help with that. You will need gum Arabic, too."

Rare as a damselfly lighting on the plume of her pen, this offer from Leopold's close friend. She should decline, but must she? She is not, after all, betrothed.

3.

Leopold's door opens before Conrad can knock. He is the first to arrive for the weekly gathering.

"Heinrich is sure to bait you again," Leopold says, standing aside so his friend can enter. "You should ignore him when he's on the attack."

"He asks questions I prefer not to answer."

"Do you have an answer? Will you fight for the Confederacy?" Leopold draws beer from a barrel. "I didn't come here to fight." Conrad sits facing the door. None of them did. He and his friends are *freidenker*, Freethinkers, compelled to leave Germany by religious and political oppression. Yet, in the place where they hoped to find freedom, they are again entangled in armed conflict.

Leopold hands him the mug of amber brew. "There will be conscription, surely. The Union protected our right to oppose owning slaves. The Confederacy does not. If you are conscripted, Con, you will be asked to kill supporters of the Union merely to keep your patron's human 'property' enslaved."

"I don't wish to kill anyone." Not even Leo understands. Conrad's work depends on patrons, and the patrons are slaveholders. Only they can afford the lavish painted decoration of their houses. If he refuses to work for them, he will never earn enough to marry.

Leopold sets down his thick glass with a thump. "I will not fight to support one man's owning another. I could not forgive myself."

"How do you propose to avoid it? You are planning marriage. When you are married, Leo, what will you do? How will you care for Johanna?" Speaking her name sends pleasurable, if distracting, eddies along his spine.

"She must accept me, first," Leopold says. "Time enough to think of it, then."

Conrad lifts his mug, leans forward to drink deeply. She has not given her answer. He must hide the stirring of hope in his chest.

4.

He has been painting the house near Trübsal for several months, room by room, preparing the surfaces, devising the appropriate designs, executing them. Simplicity in the bedrooms, more ornate decoration for public rooms. He chooses natural or geometrical images, nothing religious. No cherubs.

The family vacates each space while he works, moves back into it when he is done. He is nearing completion of the second floor parlor, the end of this commission. He considers it a race against the war, with the war winning.

Each day, he travels seven miles by road to the house, cross country in good weather to lessen the distance. Today's shortcut takes him past a cotton field, where the dark limbs of enslaved Africans churn shadow out of sunlight. It is planting time, and the men move with a relentless efficiency down the rows.

Further on, a dark-skinned woman looks up from a large iron kettle in the yard of a shanty. She is boiling laundry, much as Conrad's own Prussian mother boiled it.

Conrad has never conversed with a person in bondage, yet he, also, has plowed furrows, sowed seed on land that was not his. There are small but true commonalities between himself and these African souls. Such desperation they must have felt, torn from free lives, brought here against their will. Forced to rely on an owner's whim for adequate food and lodging, for care when they are sick.

The owners surely know how impossible it is for such injustice to endure much longer. They must greatly fear the possibility of rebellion. But how can they think this war will end well for them? They are almost certain to lose.

And he with them, if he is conscripted.

He enters the parlor from the upstairs gallery, the way future guests will do.

The room's asymmetry had been galling at first, the fireplace jammed beside one window. Centering the design on the windows themselves was the only solution. The effect depends upon his execution of the medallion on the fireplace wall, an abundance of fruit and flowers spilling from a Grecian vase. So far he is largely satisfied. Never entirely so.

The painted ceiling is framed in pale green to match the walls. A rolling vine bedecked with trumpet-shaped blossoms and curling tendrils borders the cream-colored central ground. From each midpoint of the vine's four segments, a vertical composition of classical elements in gold and blue and red points to a green parrot inside a circlet of morning glory leaves.

He has left the frieze for last. In truth, he has been delaying. The ceiling depicts a dream for the future, orderly and secure. The walls, connecting to the earth, address reality, which at the present time, embraces chaos. If he extends the rational order of classicism to the frieze, he would not be true to his concept. And this commission must reflect his best, most sincere, effort. There will be no more until the war is over.

He will be compelled to flee or fight. In either case, separated for years from what he loves.

His work.

Johanna.

For Leopold's sake, Conrad has tried to put her out of his mind. For weeks he has forced himself to look away when she comes near, although every hair on his skin rises toward her presence.

He should not have approached her while she was drawing. Should not have offered to help with supplies. The offering is a small thing, something he would do for a male friend. Only the taint of his forbidden feeling transforms this innocent act into one that verges on betrayal.

He abhors his weakness. She is beautiful, of course, and her gaze is wide. He had not expected that when he approached.

She looks beyond the practicality of the day's needs. Uses her capacity for noticing the world to make art, as he does, the art of daily life, daily experience.

She has made him understand how lonely he is.

5.

Conscription comes in spring. And enforcement.

The men gather at the home of Johanna's cousin, Ursula. Their voices converge in bravado, passing exhortations to resistance from one to the other like *Koch Kase* on pumpernickel. Johanna, serving them beer, moves quietly among their words.

"Someone's coming." A sharp note from Ursula's husband, Reinhold. Leopold breaks off in mid-sentence.

The other men around the table crane necks. Hermann rises partway in his seat for a better look.

In the yard, a lathered horse slows to a stop, ground-hitched. The rider hurrying toward them is Fritz, a fellow Lateiner from the nearby Latium community. The parlor door swings open. Fritz, gray-haired, rotund, is breathing hard. The men pull up an additional chair. Johanna brings a mug, pours.

Between swallows, he gives his news. "Eight of us, taken by force. The Guard are heading this way. You should prepare yourselves."

A sour scent arrives in the room, one of fear and masculine arousal.

"We will fight them," Leopold says. "We will support the Union."

"A man must have his freedom," says Heinrich.

"Yes, all men," says Hermann.

All men, the familiar phrase from these brave, high-minded intellectuals. And something in addition to alarm stirs inside Johanna, something quite small yet noticeable. So many of the slaves are women. Are they subsumed into "all men," as if swallowed? Is she? Do her countrymen even think of women, slave or free, when they debate the future?

They certainly never speak about what freedom means for a *frau*—the word itself signifies woman and wife interchangeably.

As presently stands, her husband, if she had one, might beat any part of Johanna's body without penalty, impregnate her against her will. If she ran away, he might legally hunt her down and punish her—a runaway wife, instead of slave, but punished all the same.

Wives remain little more than the remnant Biblical rib of the man whose name they carry. They cannot own property or vote. They lack the opportunity for formal education. Among this group of educated men, the contrast rankles doubly.

Surely, their wives have an easier life than that of enslaved Africans. This is beyond question. But freedom requires more than an absence of abuse and ownership.

Johanna herself, lacking a husband, is not owned. Even so, her legal freedom has limits. The expectations of female duty create bonds as thick and inflexible as rope.

Ursula will never allow Johanna hours in which she might study botany or make her drawings. The best she can hope for are moments alone with the few useful books she may find residing in the personal libraries of their male friends. Moments that escape the notice of her cousin and the other wives who view her aspiration as a form of immaturity verging on betrayal.

The word *Mexico* returns her attention to the men's conversation.

"The border isn't far," Leopold is saying. "Once across, we have many options."

His resonant voice dominates. How quietly the men listen. Leo expects to be heeded. How will such a man react when, as husband, he realizes that Johanna's art—which he has barely noticed so far—diverts attention from himself?

She thinks of Conrad, who accepts her seriousness of purpose. He looks at her work, at her longing, without condescension. Through his generosity she has completed two drawings in full color.

Will he depart with the others? He is working, today, but he will soon hear the news.

"Those Guard fellows are like heel-flies," Fritz is saying. "They'll hunt you down. I've heard stories."

Johanna has heard stories too. Not far from San Antonio, German men loyal to the Union have been summarily hanged as traitors.

"We must provision ourselves well," says Hermann. "Arm ourselves. It will take time."

"More time than we have." Heinrich's deep voice.

"We may rely on our women to hold them off," Leopold says.

At last, the female populace arrives in the conversation. *Unsere Frauen*: Our women.

Whose woman does she wish to be?

6.

In the solitude of a Sunday with the patron's family away at church, Conrad works steadily. The paint flows from his brush into the shapes he has chosen as surely as rounded notes rise from the strings of a violin. The air lies soft on his skin, and, through the open windows, a susurrus of birdsong proclaims its cheerful indifference to human striving.

The song stills. A horse's exhalation disturbs the silence. Someone has arrived. Then, from the yard, "Hello? Anyone?"

Her voice.

He emerges onto the gallery.

Johanna peers up at him from below, shading her eyes. She wears a brown dress and a broad-brimmed hat. "The conscriptors arrived early today. We told them the men had gone," she says. "I think they believed us."

"Have they gone? Leo? Hermann?"

"Tonight, after dark. The Guard will come this way before long."

He nods. Has she traveled here just to warn him?

"Will you go with Leo and the others?" she asks, voicing his own dilemma.

"The work isn't finished. It can't be rushed." He becomes aware of his disheveled appearance. Paint-spattered smock. Face, too, no doubt. And why is he still holding the brush in his hand?

She begins to move around the yard. A tree in vivid new leaf shades one corner. Narcissi bloom by the gate. The family dogs, who swirled briefly about her as she dismounted, now lie in the dust outside the fence. The black one raises himself to scratch an ear, then plops back down.

She has come here alone.

They are alone.

"Please, may I see?" she asks, lifting her face to him again.

"The front door is open. Come up when you like. I have to keep working." His tone is curt, but he is too breathless to correct it. Does Leo know she's here?

By the time he hears her climbing the interior stairs, he's seated once more on the scaffold, filling in the outline of a leaf. He waits for her to react. A step or two from the top of the stairs offers a good vantage point. From there his careful disguise of the room's asymmetry has its greatest success.

A sharp intake of breath. "Oh, Conrad," she says. "How beautiful!"

He swings down. Shoulder to shoulder, they contemplate the ceiling. "You see the references to a hopeful future," he says, hiding in the explanation. "Four seasons of plenty, warmth from the fire in winter, food and fecundity."

"Roses in spring," she says, removing her hat.

"Yes." He exhales slowly. "And from the parrot, longevity and wisdom. The bird faces the fireplace, and thus, also, the head of the family who will stand there on cold evenings, warming himself."

"The parrot looks skeptical. Perhaps he doubts wisdom is a likely prospect," she says with a sidelong glance.

"Better he doubt wisdom than disdain longevity," he says. Is she teasing him?

"The frieze you're working on shows much agitation." Her eyes trace the movement of the design around the room.

He stuffs his hands into the pockets of the smock. She has touched the soft center of his concern. "Do you know the beginning of Vivaldi's *L'estate*—the peace that dissolves into a passage of great disturbance?"

"Oh, yes."

"Dismay and distress are reality now for us," Conrad says. "They work their way into the design."

"Do you think of the music when you paint?"

At her smile, he relaxes a little. "Sometimes I hear it." He has never before admitted this to anyone.

Her eyes are dark sable, shining.

"You're upset by Leopold's decision to flee, aren't you?" she asks, surprising him.

"It's natural to fear for his well-being." The cautious tone returns to his voice. If she assails him, he will have no real defense.

"If Leo did not leave, he'd be forced to fight for the Confederacy," she says. "This he will never do."

"The peril is great, either way," Conrad says. "Whatever happens, the people who support slavery will continue to outnumber us after the war. Leopold and the others have their farms. Perhaps it won't be held against them to have fought for the Union."

"And you?"

"I have only my work. If I am to have a future here, I must enlist as a Confederate. If I want a wife and family." His voice wavers.

"Should you survive," she says.

"Always that."

A pause insinuates itself between them.

"I'll go with you," she says.

He stares at her.

Her cheeks color, but she holds his gaze. "If you want," she adds. "It is not unheard of. They need nurses, laundresses, cooks. Being female, I have accumulated much of the necessary experience."

"But...Leopold?" Fool he is to say this.

"I can never marry Leopold. I've told him so. It is all right, Conrad," she says, laying a hand lightly on his forearm. "I am free to marry whom I will."

II. Waldeck, Texas, 1911

7.

Johanna lives with her daughter, Sophie, while recovering from a broken ankle. She'd been replacing a shingle on the roof of the barn, higher up the slope than she realized. When she lost footing, she plopped into a yaupon bush planted years earlier by a passing bird. Sufficiently unpleasant, what with the abundance of prickly branches, but better than hard-packed clay soil. The only damage had been to her ankle, along with a few scratches, random bruises.

So, rest: The doctor's prescription. In all her seventy-odd years, she never remembers so long a period of forced inactivity as the past three weeks. Sitting with the legs up for hours at a time cannot be good for a body, but it has given her a welcome opportunity to read; and, less welcome, to think.

Sophie's three children create a pleasant commotion when they return from school. Rudi, the lively middle child, is the first boy she ever saw run with a pail of milk, oblivious to the splashing. Sophie put a quick stop to that.

Johanna feels closest to the youngest grandchild. Lizzie, the reader. The most thoughtful, and yes, inquisitive. She's the only one who seems to realize that her grandmother is a person, rather than a piece of comfy furniture that sometimes may be coaxed to sing one of the old songs.

Today, Lizzie surprised Johanna with a question about war. The child sees the newspapers, hears the adults talking. The conflict in Mexico feels disturbingly close at hand, a vulnerability of geography, if nothing else.

The question came as they'd been reading together in the spare room Johanna is using at the back of the farmhouse. *Ivanhoe* for eleven-year-old Lizzie, while Johanna escapes into *Jekyll's Color Schemes in the Flower Garden*.

So inventive, so impossible to achieve in the harsh Texas climate.

"What is war like, *Oma*?" Lizzie asked, quite rupturing the floral daydream. Not to be shrugged off, either, or deflected. Not with Lizzie.

"Let me think about it a bit, dear. You don't mind, do you?" Lizzie's questions must be answered, but carefully, taking into account the child's sensibility, here in this new, untested century. A literal *tabula rasa*, as the Lateiners used to say, a lifetime ago. Johanna's lifetime. Before the war of secession.

She tries never to think of those days, and now—in her need to respect the child's question—she cannot avoid them. Many grandparents would ignore such queries in the belief that children should be protected from all difficult truth. Johanna, however, has noticed that the bright ones, like Lizzie, infer their own interpretations from oblique or dishonest answers, and those uninformed conclusions can be more damaging.

Thus Johanna allows entry once more for the memory. For the months when death had been as real a presence as cannon smoke or the stench of putrefaction.

How quickly, though, one became accustomed to the sight of horrific bodily injury. She hadn't expected that. The repeated shock of shredded limbs, of brain matter leaking from a broken skull, constructed a layer of remove like isinglass between the sight of the wound and its effect on the viewer. She and the other nurses moved among the carnage doing whatever they could. They had so little comfort to offer.

During the brigade's withdrawal from Vicksburg, Conrad was given leave to escort Johanna and their new baby to her cousin's farm, before rejoining the unit. His captain was glad to see them go. The presence of mother and infant in such surroundings had seemed to tempt fate.

Johanna remembers fretting over how she would appear to Ursula—the bedraggled mother, her new baby, born on the outskirts of a battlefield. How could they possibly be welcomed?

And they were not.

Four of the twelve Lateiners who left for Mexico had been killed en route by militia. Ursula's husband, Reinhold, and Leopold, both dead. The immediate sorrow, even after all this time, retains its power to hollow out Johanna's spirit. Leo had been so full of life and promise. Reinhold had been so young, just months off Conrad's own age. With four children, by then.

Someone had to be blamed.

Ursula was not interested in Conrad's carefully reasoned explanation for enlisting. She did not care that he, a flautist, never fired a gun. That he, in fact, risked his life unarmed in every skirmish. These things counted for nothing. The transgression Ursula could not forgive was that he, too, had not died.

For more than a year Johanna and Sophie lived in Cousin Ursula's house, an existence defined by duty, by chores. Ursula, mired within her grief, had been incapable of the smallest pleasure. She was numb to sunsets, to wildflowers in spring, to her children's laughter. Food, for her, had no savor, and she would not allow herself strong drink.

Johanna took on all the cooking in addition to laundry and milking. She hoped the additional rest would speed her cousin's recovery. And she needed to prove herself a willing member of the household, accepting of every duty. She could risk nothing. She and Sophie needed this home while Conrad continued to serve. She must take care to stay helpful, displaying no sign of the offensive artistic impetus that had complicated her life with Ursula before she married Conrad. No sign of dormant aspirations or the desire to be different—rounder, she had thought, more complete. A woman of hues and tints, fully pig-mented as a flower.

Her need for art, for learning, however, was in no way dead, despite the war. Muffled at times, but not dead.

Lizzie, nearby, inserts a bookmark, lays *Ivanhoe* on the nearest table. A blue ribbon, holding back her fair hair, prevents it from obscuring her round, determined face. She won't let the subject go, that's obvious.

"Was it horrible, *Oma*?" she asks, in a tone that barely conceals her thrilled anticipation of gruesome detail. "Mother said you were a nurse."

"They had great need of nurses," Johanna replies. Hands were what they really needed. She'd had only the most rudimentary training. "Wartime is always horrifying, *liebchen*. I hope you will never confront it."

Lizzie, mulling this unsatisfactory answer, begins to roam around the room. She fingers Johanna's toiletries, her sketchbook, picks up her grandmother's only likeness of Conrad in its gilt and leather frame.

Please put it down. Johanna thinks the words, but doesn't say them.

"Can a person be happy while a war is going on?" Lizzie asks, studying the picture.

Perhaps the child is worried, there has been so much talk of General Villa, the capture of Cíudad Juarez. One can never be sure how much is overheard, misunderstood, or understood too well. Johanna shifts a little on the settee, rearranges the blanket over her bandaged ankle.

"Happiness is always occasional, *liebchen.*"

Lizzie looks puzzled.

Johanna searches for a familiar example. "You know the *stollen* your mother makes at Christmas? How there are morsels of glacéed fruit scattered through the bread?"

The child nods slowly, sensing an evasion.

"So, then, happiness is like finding a little piece of fruit when you least expect it."

A small pucker arrives between Lizzie's fair eyebrows. "I am not fond of glacéed fruit, *Oma.*"

A devotee of the literal, this child. Perhaps she will outgrow it.

"What I'm saying, *liebchen,* is that happiness is not a feeling of long duration, as the stories we read suggest. 'And they lived happily ever after.' No, it comes when you least expect it—a brilliant sunset after a week of gray days, for instance. Even during the war, we had a happy moment or two. When we knew we were having a baby."

A partial truth. Making the baby had been happy. Knowing she was pregnant had been more like panic.

"You mean Mama?"

"Yes. Our darling Sophie."

Lizzie returns the picture to the table with the toiletries, then perches on the edge of the settee, momentary as a chickadee on a branch.

"You were happier before the war, then?"

Johanna sighs. It is surely perverse of her to feel melancholy when asked to recall happiness. "You know the Towsons' old stagecoach stopping place on the way to Bernheim."

"Mama said that's where the man stayed when he came through to collect your drawings."

"Herr Lindheimer stayed there, yes. My house was too small, and it would not have been seemly."

"Did he give them back?" Oh, her round, quizzical eyes. Cobalt blue.

"The drawings?"

Lizzie nods.

"I have some drawings, yes," Johanna says. Boxes of them under her bed at home. Other drawings stacked in a cedar chest in the attic where Sophie and Lizzie will find them after she is gone.

Lizzie reflects for a moment. "Did you like having your drawings in a book, *Oma*? Did that make you happy?"

"They bought supper for your mother and me. Weeks of supper, and two pairs of shoes. But, no, not happy, exactly. A sense of accomplishment."

Lizzie looks away, disappointment clear in the tilt of her chin. Her elders bend her already toward accomplishment. Embroidery, needlepoint, playing the violin. Sometimes drawing, too. Johanna has detected the presence of duty in her granddaughter's activities, but not truly pleasure. Lizzie may be one of the world's souls for whom happiness remains elusive.

"Please tell me, *Oma*."

Outside the window, a wren scrabbles in the flower box, beginning the new cycle. Johanna removes her spectacles, rubs the irritated place on her nose where they normally rest, then wipes the lenses with her handkerchief before securing the earpieces once more.

"You know your *Opa* was a decorative painter. He'd been painting the parlor ceiling of Mr. Towson's house. It belonged to another family then."

Lizzie nods. She's familiar with the outline of the story.

"He was showing it to me one day—an especially beautiful design, I thought. He and I were standing alone in the room admiring his work. And each other." Johanna smiles, shaking her head. "I was very young. We both were. We were discovering what we felt about one another and it was like a wall fell away, and there we were, with every possibility stretching out before us. The future seemed endless, you know, an endless bright place."

"And you were happy."

"Yes, I've never had a happier moment."

Lizzie is kneeling on the floor, now, her elbows on the cushion of the settee.

"But the war came."

"That's right, and we went through it together."

Thoughts fly across her granddaughter's expressive face. "Is the ceiling still there? Can we go see it?"

"We'd have to get permission from the owner."

"Don't you want to see it again, *Oma?*"

A vague odor of fresh paint infuses her mental image of the ceiling with the memory of Conrad's presence. To see it now without him?

"I'm...not really sure, *liebchen.*"

III. Galveston, Texas

8. 1865

Conrad sits on the edge of the long splintery pier, removes his boots, peels off his socks. They're bloody, but not as bad as he'd feared after hours of walking, wandering the city. Three weeks here have not diminished his amazement at the chaos, although it might well have been predicted for a port city after the war.

More than for himself, he deplores the effect of the place on Johanna and their daughter, Sophie. The streets are filthy. Drunken men lurch about and accost respectable women. He and Johanna have very little money. No one has much.

He spends hours every day visiting the German clubs in search of commissions. To attract interest, he must put himself forward in the manner a salesman does, never easy, much harder now.

His nerves, shredded fine as dandelion fluff, betray his fragility. He startles at the slightest loud noise. On Saturday nights when men outside saloons fire their pistols into the air, he cowers in bed and hopes she does not think too much less of him.

Some days, he thinks of plunging into the sandy gray Gulf waters, presently lapping at the pier's supports ten feet below him. A restful sound. It's only the reality of Johanna and Sophie that keeps him dry. The world is not kind to unprotected females. He will not willingly desert them.

They have already endured so much. The lines of sadness around Johanna's eyes and mouth are because of him. He should never have allowed her to accompany him to the war. In reality, he'd been stupefied that a woman would desire the experience.

Such suffering she has witnessed—they have witnessed—pumping cataracts of blood, scorched faces, constant pestilence. If miracles were real, the miracle would be that he, she and the child have emerged whole, or nearly so.

He picks up a drying sock, where the bleeding from his blisters has begun to crust. He had been foolish to believe he could plan for the future with a war going on. Stupid to think that anything familiar would survive, much less a complex society once the institution supporting it had been swept away.

The practicality he tried to live by revealed itself to be as fully idealistic as any one of Leopold's iron abstractions. As fully useless, blown to dust by passion and blood memory.

He has failed most painfully in his drive to protect his

talent, make a safe place for his work, for family life. His family, in the current circumstance, lacks any of the security he had intended to create.

He must find a patron, find work.

If only he retains his facility. These hands and fingers, blunted by scrambling over mud and rock, dragging wounded comrades off the field, digging into abandoned gardens for the overlooked turnip or potato or onion—he'd been so hungry at times—these hands must be capable of delicate embellishments, executed with exactitude.

And what will he discover when he begins to work? The surfaces in this salty, humid air may not be amenable to decoration. The wood in new buildings may be imperfectly cured. Wood must release the greenness of its life that clings so tightly to each fiber, or the paint will not withstand the material's shrinkage over time. The decoration itself will flake and be lost. Green wood causes much heartache.

So many unknowns.

And yet, the feel of the surface to the brush, the creamy texture, the silken ease when it goes well. The exhilaration when all elements come together. These memories are when the beat of his heart quickens, when all seems as if it must be possible once more.

For her, too. When he is earning again, she will have time to paint. The wildflowers of this barrier island must struggle to populate, but they survive. She has given him so much—love, her youth, their daughter. Foresworn her art to care for him and Sophie.

He slides the socks, dry enough, over his battered feet, puts on his boots and rises. He will ignore the pain for as long as it takes to walk home. Johanna will dress his blisters, render him sufficiently restored to withstand tomorrow's search.

Overhead a chevron of brown pelicans soars lazily eastward ahead of storm clouds that roil ever higher in the west. For a moment, breaking through, the sun spills glittering coins across the formerly leaden waves.

Reliable alchemy.

Such beauty inhabits the everyday, comprised of threat withheld.

9. 1867

The sound is not quite human, in the way an infant's initial warning mimics a rasp, to be followed by the full-throated cry that will come. And does not, now, come, however much she wishes it might to release her husband's pain toward healing, instead of merely rushing on, a whirring hum behind compressed lips and his face so hot that a cool cloth quickly loses its utility.

His legs weave patterns across the sheet. They are never still. He had commented upon rising this morning that his head ached. His tone was mildly curious, unconcerned. The weakness that flattened him came an hour later, then the chills so severe that the vibration of the bed shook a drawing from the wall, one she especially loves, of a parrot with a bold eye, Conrad's own eye.

Johanna pulls away at that thought, although her body remains close, adding quilts or removing them as the chills come and go. Her hands squeeze out the cloths, lay them on his brow, replace them when they match his skin for heat. Her hands, her body operate without her inner participation.

She is somewhere above the tableau, up in the corner, perhaps, looking down, or higher so that she can see Sairey in the kitchen with Sophie and the new baby, as far away from this room as possible in the house. Sairey had the yellow fever as a child and lived. They say if you do, you will never have it again.

She rises further, away from the reminder that many do not live. Already on their street, two have died out of the seven that are ill. Eight, now, with Conrad. She must surmount these thoughts so that they will not acquire substance.

Now is what matters. Only now.

Wolf Moon

I.

Maggie slides onto one of the upright wooden chairs at the café a block from her apartment in lower Manhattan. The waiter brings her usual—Earl Grey tea and a warm croissant. Normally he stops to chat, but not today, and she sits there wondering whether her nine o'clock will no-show again.

She takes a cautious sip of the hot liquid, easing into the moment, when she realizes she's looking at Liam across the room, deep in conversation with a bearded man.

It's Liam's dear head, the short blond hair the way he wore it in middle school. She's seeing the back of him, of course, and part of one side, an ear and the slope of cheek to jaw. Her breath comes more quickly with each familiar detail, it feels so good to have him near.

II.

Liam is seven when the Donovans move from New York to rural Texas in the late eighties. Twenty acres in a hilly area halfway between Houston and Austin. A few animals for the kids, Denny says. A pony, dogs. Got that. Got more, actually—a goat, chickens, two cows. Maggie knows nothing about such creatures. Denny's the one who spent summers on an uncle's south Texas ranch. Happy summers, which are why the family is here, instead of in Houston, where Denny works.

From the start, though, they're under attack: Fire ants in the bathwater, copperheads in the flower bed, scorpions in the closet. And, one day in the backyard, a rabid raccoon.

The sick creature lurches out of the woods at dusk on a Friday in August and bites Liam when he, stupidly, prods it with a stick. His sister, Abby, nails the animal with a 20-gauge. There are five shotguns in the house by then, each one a different bore. Denny had been teaching Abby on the .410. "Nice little varmint gun," he calls it.

There's more kick to a 20-gauge, but thirteen-year-old Abby doesn't miss, even with her friend Kazie crouched on the pool storage box, yelling at her to blow it away.

Liam huddles in the prickly grass, holding his arm. Tears soak the collar of his shirt, but he doesn't make a sound.

Maggie kneels beside him. "Come on, sweetie, I know it hurts, but you'll be okay." Sure, he will. The hospital will have a protocol for this kind of thing. Before that, though, there's the dead animal. Maggie will need to handle it. Everyone, including the dogs, must stay clear of where it died. There'll be infected blood and bits of tainted flesh in the grass and dirt.

She keeps Liam close as they hurry into the house to clean the wound.

Through a window she spots Abby in the den with the gun—please God, locking the case. Kazie will be matching her step for step. Such an intensity to friendships at that age. For Maggie, there was Lila in ninth grade, pale Lila of the black eyes and buzzing hive of male attention.

Sometimes, of course, those friendships don't end in a season. They go on to alter lives in ways no parent can predict.

For the first part of the ride to the ER, Liam stares ahead, expressionless. His father's always telling him to hang tough, whatever that means for a seven-year-old. Denny isn't around much to explain. The new job keeps him at work until after eight most evenings. Family activities wait for weekends. Farm chores, too, the ones Maggie can't do alone. By then, she has a long list that would discourage anyone. Maybe that's what she intends.

The disgusting carcass rides in a plastic bag in the trunk. Kazie knew exactly what to do. No surprise. She has grown up here. Her family lives one gate over, although Maggie has never met them, not even the mother.

The local mothers she has met are friendly enough, but cautious. "They consider you a Yankee," Denny says, like it's to be expected, and maybe it is.

In a Houston school, differences would disappear into a crazy-quilt of variation, but Denny refuses. "Too much driving," he says, though Maggie would be doing most of it.

"They're smart kids," he tells her. "Coming from a small town will improve their chance of a good college. Schools have quotas, you know."

The idea of gaming the college application process irritates her, but Denny's been selling Texas from the start. Piling up reasons why this move is good for all of them. Her resistance holds no more significance than a fallen tree blocking his way. Removal is his answer, not trying to find out why it fell.

Liam makes a soft, pinched noise, low in his throat, and shifts position in the seat beside her.

"Hang on, sweetie. We're almost there." She can see *Emergency* pulsing red above the cars that throng the parking lot. Will Denny meet them? Will he have checked his voicemail?

Apparently not.

"You should have been there," she scolds him later, after Liam—inoculated, bandaged—is asleep. Denny sits astride a stool in the kitchen, sipping a vodka while she cuts a slice of hot freezer pizza. He gives her the wide-eyed sincere gaze she once found flattering.

"But you had it handled, Babe, didn't you?"

*

By mid-January, Kazie's struggling. An older boy named Jonah cruises Abby's locker between classes. Tall, with straight brown hair he keeps flipping away from his face. When Kazie sees Abby smiling back at him, it's like a wind sprint session that lasts one interval too long, that aching absence of breath.

Kazie loves Abby, really loves, way more than a best friend, or at least differently, in a different part of her heart and self. She lies in bed at night and thinks about how great it would be if...if what? There's this enormous wall between what she feels and what she can imagine actually happening. Like the side of a building, the back side, tall, with no windows.

Abby's always talking about Jonah—his dark eyes, the way his smile tilts down on one side. Kazie can tell when a dude is hot, but she doesn't feel it, really, not like Abby does. Maybe she's just slow. She's heard her mother, Dawn, say that on the phone. Not ready for boys yet. Is that possible?

Kazie would like an answer, but Dawn's been wasted ever since she cut Wayne loose last month. She never used to drink. Maybe if Ray hadn't died—but he did. Blow-outs happen, Dawn said. Offshore rigs are never safe. As if that made losing your dad something a person could prepare for.

Wayne started hanging around way too quick after the accident. He was a sharp dresser, give him that, but the lizardy kind, slick and shiny. Within weeks, Dawn became this overage *chica* in tight jeans and barn red hair, off dancing every other night.

When Wayne's 350 spun ten-inch ruts into the front yard after their last big fight, Kazie figured things would get back to normal. As normal as they could be without her dad. But Dawn just spends all day in her sleep-shirt in front of the TV, and it's a lie that vodka has no smell.

*

In the deceptive light of a February dusk, Maggie and Liam stop on the side of a county road after his second skating party that week. Sated with cake and two hours of steady seven-year-old screaming, he's asleep in the back seat, plugged into his Walkman. She's grateful for a few moments to recover.

She lowers the window. Beyond the barbed wire fence, rolling farmland opens out, dotted with green smudges of mercury vapor lights. Cold, still air thrums in her ears. All she sees of the rising moon, so far, is a lambent haze behind the Wiebers' barn. It's the Wolf Moon, this month, when nothing is expected to grow. In her yard, though, the pear tree is wrapped in white blossoms. Redbuds exhale a pink mist along the fence. Pretty, but disorienting. Even winter, here, can't be relied on.

Denny keeps saying it'll get easier when he's not traveling so much. Maggie wants to believe that. She loves her family. The animals, too, especially the pony nobody rides. It's everything else that feels like a foreign country.

On their very first day, slowing for the turn to the house, "Gross, Mom, look! That's gross!" Liam was pointing at seven coyotes in ascending levels of decomposition, hanging by their heads from the neighbor's fence. She closed her eyes, but not before the image struck of the last one, shreds of skin dangling from a skull to which one ear and patches of pelt were still attached.

"They're predators," Denny explained, as she fought back nausea. "They kill chickens, newborn calves. People here are realistic about nature. Shooting is part of the life."

He meant it's a normal thing, the way it's normal for him to have six firearms around the house. Their ongoing argument.

"I hear you," Denny says when she protests, although he doesn't, really. He believes gun safety rules remove the household danger. He's always so sure about things. In their early days, she had thrilled to his confidence. She'd felt sheltered, confirmed in her femininity, as though she'd been waiting for a man to draw her into his warmth and carry her along.

During the year she was studying Lila's every move, Maggie had despaired of ever connecting in that way. Boys came so easily to Lila. Even older boys grew helpless in the glow of her face turned up to them. Maggie watched, unsuccessfully, to see what drew them in. Maybe that's what Kazie is doing with Abby. Trying to learn from a peer what ought to be innate. It's a simple explanation, although the older her children get, the more Maggie finds complexity in every interaction.

In the parked car, she can hear the faint, high-pitched susurrus of Liam's earphones. At last, the bright orb of the moon slips free of the barn, and hovers over it huge and mysterious and yellow as a Macy's balloon. The girl who longed to be shaped by her husband now wonders what it would be like to have no tether, to fly away across the world in pursuit of a dream.

Or just to Seattle, where Denny is tonight, a bi-weekly business trip for the past three months. One overnight each time, grown lately to three. He keeps apologizing. The client is ramping up, he says, to launch something called a website. Maggie would understand the pressure if she'd ever held a corporate job.

Would she, though? If, instead of bookselling on Third Avenue, she'd given up, say, a banking career to follow him to Texas? Would that make her any happier in a place where she has barnyard animals to feed, and no one to talk to about it, except a husband who's rarely home?

"I used to be competent," she told him, the night before he left. She was folding towels, while he brushed his teeth.

Denny spat, glanced up at her reflection in the mirror. "Maggie, don't."

"I had a job I was good at. We made it work."

"You know you'll figure this out. You've got be flexible, sweetheart."

*

Today, for the first time all year, Kazie sits alone at lunch. With every wrong person who comes through the line, the empty seat beside her sinks further into the cafeteria floor. She has to grip the table edge to keep from sliding after it. Only when she gets up to leave for class does she see Abby on the other side of the room, eating with Jonah. Her eyes catch Abby's for a split second before Abby glances away.

Kazie waits inside the restroom where Abby always stops before class. She tucks her jaw-length hair—impossibly straight—behind her ears. Slips it free again. She rubs Chapstick on her lips, like it's lip gloss. Girls who aren't Abby come in. Go out, chattering. Kazie's hands are trembling as she puts her comb away.

The door opens. Abby sees Kazie in front of the mirror, looks embarrassed for half a second, pivots in place and is gone.

In the nearest stall, someone has left a used tampon floating in the toilet. Kazie sits down anyway and shuts her eyes. Her thoughts, half-formed, keep erasing themselves, until she's not thinking of anything, at all.

After basketball practice that afternoon, Coach Lennon stops her at the locker room door. "Anything wrong, hon? You seemed a little unfocused out there."

Coach may be younger than Kazie's mom, but she has the same smoker's wrinkles around her mouth. Her blue eyes are kind. "You can talk to me, if you need to. I'm good at keeping secrets."

But where would Kazie start? Sports aside, her whole life is a secret. How does that come off, a person entirely made up of secrets? Are you like all mysterious and interesting, or are you just frigging invisible? In the hallways, she watches to see if anyone notices her, makes eye contact. Away from the gym, they don't. So, if no one sees you, does that mean you're not really there?

The thought skitters along her nerves like a mouse in

the wall. She has to pinch herself hard on the soft under-side of her arm to make it go away.

That night, Kazie chips at a package of thickly fatted frozen tamales with a kitchen knife. On booze runs, Dawn occasionally remembers to buy food. Mostly, though, Kazie drives the pickup to the store so there'll be something she can nuke or toast. She's too young for a license, but her dad taught her the fundamentals on their tractor.

Two months ago she would have told Abby about it, like breaking the law in this small, necessary way was some kind of ballsy thing.

A final jab of the knife blade dislodges two tamales, still stuck together, and Kazie nukes them on a paper towel. It's late and she's starving.

She's been waiting to see if her mother would eat with her, but Dawn's snoring on the couch. Her dyed red hair has grown out gray at the roots, and a little drool from her open mouth pools into a dark blot on the cushion, a speech balloon for when there's nothing left to say.

Kazie shucks the tamales onto a clean paper towel and carries them outside. Overhead, the full moon stares down with its off-center face.

Patches of rust make the table look dirty in the moon-light. Every spring Ray would paint the outdoor furniture, fertilize the lawn, do repairs. From here his workshop in the corner of the yard looks just like he left it, but inside the room humid dust congeals on the tools, paint thickens in the cans. He'd taught Kazie how to swing a hammer and use a level, but he died before he could teach her enough of what she needs to know. Not just about taking care of the place, although Dawn's helpless that way. But about how to be in the world, how to stay alive, and why.

At the funeral, his coffin was closed, and she'd been afraid to ask exactly what was inside, what had been recovered after the explosion. She kept thinking he was out there, still, at his workbench. She could smell his sweat. And although she liked to imagine him hanging around the yard, it took months before she'd peer into a workshop window—she was too scared of what she'd see, and of what she wouldn't.

She jams the paper towel, limp with grease, into her jacket pocket. The longer she sits at the table, the more the moonlight pours truth over all of it, the yard, the house, her mom. Her. It's a hopeless kind of truth that pushes her upright into her own pale shadow.

Her feet, on this cool bright night, propel her down to the gate, across the pasture, along the path she's worn to where she wants to be.

Abby's yard is deserted at this hour. A second moon wobbles in the dark rectangle of the swimming pool. The cushion of the lounge chair is damp and Kazie pulls up her hood, tucks her hands into her pockets. She thought it would be better here, but it's not. Same moon. Same alone. She closes her eyes.

A crunch of gravel and somebody's car pulls into the driveway. No lights. Kazie rolls off the chair and scrunches down beside it. The stone of the deck is hard against her bony knees.

Almost immediately, the side door to the house opens and Abby comes out, walking fast. The passenger door to the car swings shut behind her.

It's like when the basketball catches you in the stomach. Kazie can't breathe. She can't see inside the car, Jonah's car, but the curve of its fender is clear and sharp in the moonlight.

What are they doing? Don't think about that.

The moon inches onward.

At last, Abby jumps out and runs to the house. The car grinds slowly up the drive to the road.

The house is dark. Abby's room goes dark. Security lights drop yellow circles onto the shrubbery.

Kazie tries the side door and it's open.

*

Maggie wakes in the night to Bailey's low growl. Brie, their arthritic Lab, is breathing audibly on her bed in the corner, but the terrier is staring, stiff-legged, at the door. It's nearly two a.m. The alarm readout shows the side door is open, but Denny won't be home until Friday. Did one of the kids go out? Would the dog even notice that kind of thing?

She hesitates. The handgun Denny keeps in the bedside drawer scares her, but she's more afraid of what the dark country night disguises.

While Bailey plunges down the stairs, she confirms that Abby's in her room. Liam's sleepy face appears in his doorway. "Mom, what's going on?"

"Bailey thinks he heard something. Get back inside and close the door."

She inches down the staircase, pointing the heavy weapon at the floor. That's right, isn't it? Denny taught her the basics, but she has only fired the gun a couple of times.

Amber light from an outdoor flood spills into the empty hallway. The breakfast room door stands ajar. Did Bailey go out? The only sound is the purr of the refrigerator in the kitchen.

No.

Something just clicked, something metallic.

She curls her index finger around the trigger and raises the revolver level with her ear, pointing up, the way they do in police procedurals. Does a cop feel like this? Terrified and powerful?

She approaches the entrance to the library, double doors they never close. Her heartbeat moves into her throat. She presses her side to the frame and peeks around into the room. Nothing out of place that she can see.

She swallows, relaxes a little. Where is that dog? She flicks on the light.

The gun case is open.

A hooded figure springs up from behind the sofa. The shape of a shotgun in the intruder's hands is unmistakable.

Maggie's finger is already pulling the trigger when she recognizes Kazie.

Both guns go off and the night explodes into swirling bits of sheetrock. Liam appears out of nowhere in the middle of it, his head frosted with dust.

Abby arrives moments later, screaming surely, although Maggie can't really hear it.

Somewhere under the debris, Kazie lies, bleeding. The paramedics come and stabilize her, send her by Life-Flight to Houston.

Through it all, Maggie's mind flips from one blurry image to another, like a TV screen from her childhood with the vertical hold slipping: Her fear in the hallway, the looming figure, the little globules of dust stuck to Liam's lashes.

He must have seen everything. Seen Kazie rise with the shotgun in her hands and Maggie pointing the revolver at his sister's best friend. But how can anyone know with certainty which of them fired first?

In the room, an acrid smell lingers, of human excrement and something burnt. Such a horrible thing cannot have happened. It must be undone, time rolled back. Answers must be found, answers that make sense of it, that make it go away.

But there are only questions. What was Kazie doing there at that hour? The gun case should have been locked. Denny never uses the ten-gauge, his biggest bore. What had the girl been planning to do?

In the days that follow, the sheriff interrogates everyone. But no, it wasn't a break-in. Kazie comes and goes frequently, although not usually at 2AM.

Had she been depressed? School counselors are particularly interested in that one. Kazie's Mom doesn't think so, and when Kazie is well enough to answer questions, she tells them she remembers nothing about that night. Nothing.

Abby can't help, either. No matter who asks, she begins to cry.

Maggie blames Denny and his guns.

"Get rid of them," she tells him. "Get rid of them, or I will."

When she says it, they are standing by the kitchen door, his well-worn carry-on slumped on the floor beside them. It's the fifth day after the accident, with Kazie still in the ICU. Despite that, he'll be flying out at noon, a quick turnaround, this time. An emergency, he says.

Emergency. Right.

Maggie shot a human being, for Christ's sake, a child. If there had been no weapons around, it would never have happened.

"The guns are my responsibility, Maggie," Denny says.

"Yes, but you're leaving." She doesn't want him to stay. She wants him to argue, give her an opening through which her rage can batter him.

Too late, though, too late on every count.

He picks up the suitcase. "Those guns belonged to my father, Maggie. They're worth thousands."

And his tone is so uninflected that she understands he isn't trying to provoke her. He simply doesn't see her anger or fear or remorse as anything that matters very much. Even now, with the neighbor's daughter in intensive care, he can't see more than the mess he finds inevitable when women are involved.

III.

The following years fall upon them, one after another, the way it goes. Kazie and her Mom move to a little town outside Dallas. Abby doubles down on schoolwork, graduating second in her class.

Maggie and Denny are divorced, after a four-year slog. He marries, and eventually divorces, the woman he had been seeing in Seattle. The perfect wife is hard to find, it seems.

And Liam?

Sweet-faced Liam turns angry in his teenage years. His wheat gold hair falls unwashed across his forehead, hiding and causing pimples. His gray-green gaze travels inward. More than once, he punches a window into shards; puts his fist through the bedroom wall. Maggie hears him in the late afternoon blowing holes in targets at the shooting range Denny built near the creek long before the accident.

Liam is never violent toward her, or Abby. Just silent. All boys that age are silent to some degree, aren't they? Loners, too, unless they travel in packs. Maggie learned young to avoid male teens in packs, the stares and muttered comments that surely fingered her body's tender parts.

She knew less about the solitary boys. She had no context for Liam, no frame into which he could fit and be seen. No clue about what kind of intervention, if any, might work, or if intervention, in fact, was necessary.

Surely he knows she didn't hurt Kazie on purpose. He couldn't have felt the missed heartbeat of time in which an armed stranger turned into her daughter's friend, a gap so similar to the lag between stubbing your toe and feeling the pain.

Would it have helped if she'd talked to him about that night? If she'd described the disembodied sensation of watching yourself like you were a character in a film, and the script compelled your finger to complete the act it had begun?

Would talking have changed anything?

She decides, later, that any mother might have missed the signs. Those are the years when a stranger absorbs into himself the child a mother knows and loves. And, much too soon, this transitional being makes unalterable life decisions. At eighteen a boy can buy a gun. A legal gun. An assault rifle. More than one, if he has the money.

Liam's teenage fascination with weapons of war and video combat games might have signaled only a difficult passage to manhood, the kind most boys survive. Or it might have pointed to a horrifying disaster, a mass shooting of the kind that became prevalent later.

Instead, in 2002, at nineteen, he joined the Marines. It made the kind of sense that she should have seen coming. "It's what I've always wanted to do," he told her. "Nine-eleven sealed the deal."

There was nothing Maggie could do to stop him.

IV.

If you ask her now, Maggie will say she likes her life in New York. It's fine, she'll say, and she'll mean it for most of the day. The nights aren't so bad, either, the early parts when she meets a friend for drinks or a meal—thick lentil soup, perhaps. Conversation, sometimes a movie, a play or concert—all the things she thought she missed about the city.

Then home.

A little wave to Jorge at the door. "Have a good night." Her heels clicking across the black and white marble floor. The interior of the small elevator is polished wood, some exotic variety with a bit too much red for her taste. No mirror to give the illusion of space.

Manhattan encourages illusion, though. Storefront and subway windows play consistent games of perception. Sooner or later you see everyone you've loved, for just the briefest flicker of a synapse.

Sometimes, the person she sees is Abby, waiting for a light to change. Abby, who lives in Sausalito, about as far away as she can be without dropping off the edge of the continent.

They talk, occasionally, or Skype. Only once has Abby referred to the night of the shooting—last year, when she mentioned she'd had a letter from Kazie, an actual letter, written in longhand with a stamp. Kazie was apologizing for the trouble she'd caused.

"The ninth step," Abby said, "that would be my guess."

Whether Abby has personal reasons for knowing the twelve steps of recovery, Maggie can't bring herself to ask. The closeness that would allow such questions to an adult daughter has never developed.

Trying to understand why is one reason Maggie went back to school, got her master's in clinical psych. She'd done it out of hope that studying what she'd failed at might open it to her, at last. People, that is. Families.

So far, she has failed in that, too, but at least she's helping others.

In a way, Liam's deployment brought him closer to her than he'd been since childhood. Hardly an hour could elapse without her visualizing him on the other side of the world, in villages and city streets rife with horror. Exploding IEDs, toxic chemical clouds, our own falling bombs. Those were the years when they began to use drones, guided by kids at consoles in Nevada. She has two RPA pilots in her therapy group, as surely suffering from PTSD as any more conventional warrior.

There was no place in any of it where she could know Liam would be safe.

Every time she began to relax into an ordinary pleasure, a film or simple conversation with a friend, the pang of knowing, and not knowing, would come, until it became a continuous sensation, like a hum or a buzz, far inside a wall where no source could be located and removed. A spiritual tinnitus, perhaps, that would be with her always, now.

His last day is as clear to her as if she'd been there. He was on patrol, they told her, in a barren village with a name she wishes she'd never learned to spell. He and another Marine were clearing an alley after a firefight. Their adrenaline would have been surging, hearts thumping. This kind of action was never routine, the captain explained.

That day, a young woman emerged without warning from the black hole of a doorway into blinding white heat. She carried a basket and wore a hijab, so very similar to a hoodie. And just as his startled buddy swung his weapon reflexively to fire, Liam stepped forward, into the brightness between them.

For years afterwards, Maggie would find herself thinking of Kazie. If Abby was right about the letter's purpose, Kazie had substance abuse issues. Maybe she would have had them anyway—the family had been nonfunctional at the time, Maggie learned later. But how about Maggie's own family? The faithless husband, the whiny wife, the two children who had been scarred by violence arriving in their midst without notice. Random violence, unthinkable until it happened.

Apologies—amends—were quite beside the point.

Even so, it's not surprising that sometimes Kazie comes to her in dreams, wearing that stupid hoodie. She knows it's Kazie, although she never quite sees the face.

"I forgive you, Mrs. D.," the girl says in the voice Maggie remembers from long ago, a voice so much like Liam's was, back then.

"I forgive you," Kazie says.

And it's all Maggie can do, even in the dream, not to slap her.

Cicadas

They met at the Houston museum, in front of Albert Bierstadt's Valley of the Yosemite, on loan from the M.F.A., Boston. She almost hadn't come. The painting was a reminder of the time in her life when beautiful objects gave easy pleasure. She feared its radiance might seem alien, now, disturbing.

But she was wrong. The glow spilled out of the canvas, enveloped her. Basking, she shifted from one pinched foot to the other. She hardly ever wore heels anymore.

The man appeared beside her, a little too close. "You know it's a lie," he said. "No way it really looked like that."

She edged away, offended at having her communion interrupted. He wore jeans, a corduroy jacket and faded purple t-shirt—rumpled, but clean. An academic, Lily guessed.

He kept talking.

"A landscape painting pretends to freeze time," he said, "but the scene constantly changes. Bierstadt had to reach for the memory of what he had just been looking at. Strain for it. There's a big temptation to fake intensity.

You see that in amateur work—garish purples, acid greens.
It makes me puke."

She didn't like those paintings either, but she avoided
the places where they'd be. Parking lot art shows, for
instance.

"I'm Emory Dahlgren," he said and stuck out his hand.

Lily recognized the name. She had flipped through a
catalogue of his work a few years ago, at the office of the
university press she was connected to at the time. His
paintings had been a challenge to the designer, stretching in slim, wide bands across the slick pages. In several,
repeating clusters of tiny people appeared against a landscape whose only change, as the eye moved left to right,
was the shifting angle of sunlight. "Chasing time" was
how the writer described it.

"It's us, you see," Emory said. "We try to preserve the
moment, but we can't make it live again."

"And this is the work you choose to do?" Her prick-
ing of interest in this man made no sense. Whatever she
thought of his art, he was too old, too beaten up.

"All of it's a con to some degree." He shrugged. The
lines in his thin face sloped down. Lank strands of graying
dark hair slid forward. He pushed them back. He took a
swallow of his Coke. "I don't usually come to this kind of
thing," he added, "unless it's one of mine."

She must have looked quizzical.

"I've been working a lot," he said. "I figured if I didn't
have contact with some semi-normal people, soon, I'd
forget how to be human."

He told her later he hadn't been working. He'd been in

rehab—from alcohol, not drugs. He took particular care to point that out. He was afraid of drugs.

When they met, Lily had been a widow for eight years, with an established business selling refurbished country antiques. She'd begun in her usual haphazard way, with a homely table she found in a roadside junk shop. Almost Shaker plain, it had a broken leg held together with duct tape. Someone had gouged L+J into one corner of the top.

Lily saw stories layered into the damage—a lovesick boy in overalls with a sharp penknife; years later, an angry husband the night his crop was ruined. Her heart beat faster the longer she looked. It was the idea of it, that human passion could be preserved this way in ordinary combustible wood.

Once she had begun noticing, she discovered cast-off pieces everywhere, handmade, but abused.

There were buildings, too. Farmhouses, sheds, squatting in the heat with sloping metal roofs that gleamed in the parts rust hadn't taken. Some had empty windows and walls of weathered wood chewed across the bottom as if by small animals.

Driving past a deserted house one day, she pictured the farm wife who'd lived there. She saw a wiry woman, prematurely aged, carrying water from the well her man had dug by hand. Scrubbing on a washboard the clothes whose material she'd spun herself. Women like that had worked in the fields, then cooked endless meals from what the land could render. They'd given birth to children, lost them and husbands to disease and ceaseless struggle.

The road before her blurred. She pulled over to the grassy verge, wiped her eyes. The heat of her own loss remained alive, banked, requiring only the slightest puff of her attention to renew its ache.

Anger was healthier. She felt it pulsing now. How could the dwellings that bore witness to such exhausted love and pain be discarded like the beer cans and Big Gulps lying in a roadside ditch?

Lily bought three of the dilapidated houses—for practically no money—and moved them to the patch of woods and pasture where she'd been living since Travis died. She had them painted in soft neutral colors, inside and out, and left them beside one another in a clearing, separated from her house by a hundred feet of yaupon and post oak. She used one for storing rebuilt furniture, but for the other two, she had no plan, at first.

She told Emory about the project over lunch. They'd begun meeting like that when she came to Houston. Totally casual, never a "date," by any measure.

"I've always imagined myself in that rolling countryside," he said. The lines in his face softened. "It reminds me of Wyeth country in Pennsylvania."

Emory admired Andrew Wyeth far more than most members of the art establishment admitted to. She could see the influence in details of his paintings, the way light got tangled up in gauzy curtains or in the filaments of spider webs on worn fences. Maybe Emory was also hinting—rather broadly—at his own availability. He was living, then, in a garage apartment.

She felt sorry for a person of his sensibility in that situation—lonely, trying to recover his sobriety. "One of the houses has a bathroom and kitchenette. Why don't you take it? No strings," she said.

Her words slotted into place like the tumblers in a heavy old lock. Emory wasn't the kind of man who would disturb her emotional equilibrium. If she considered him any kind of threat, she wouldn't be having lunch with him.

He accepted quickly.

Fairly soon after he moved in, Lily realized that a glint from the window of his truck was visible through the trees at certain hours of the day when he came or went. She made a point of not looking.

Lily was six when she brought home the first tiny objects of transient beauty, a mica-studded pebble from the neighbor's driveway, a Chinese tallow leaf of unsullied crimson floating in the grass. Pebbles and leaves never pretended to be more than they were. If one disappeared for reasons nobody talked about, there were always others to replace it.

Her mother, Ann, had died the previous fall, so long ago now that Lily could visualize her healthy self only from photographs. Even in snapshots, Ann looked glamorous—in a Liz Taylor sort of way, friends said, exaggerating out of sympathy, perhaps. By the time they said that, the photos had begun to fade. Her mother had faded, too, the color going first, and then the skin along her bare forearms puckering. And all the while, no one explained a thing. Not even her aunt would speak the word "cancer."

During college Lily became fascinated with the old glass bottles she saw in flea markets. She looked for ones in jewel tones, sapphire or emerald, and she arranged them wherever she could find a horizontal surface that caught a few hours of sunlight. There was such an active trade in bottles that she began to think she might deal in collectibles after graduation. She was a design major and understood already that additional income would be welcome. On the other hand, it was a precarious business. The stock she bought might not sell.

The decision to marry Travis, a year or two later, removed that problem. He was very good-looking in a firm-jawed WASPy way. Being near him caused her heart to race with pleasurable excitement. She'd felt stirrings like this before, but now she felt safe enough to let it develop, deepen.

He was securely employed. His income as an attorney gave her the freedom to work irregularly, designing books freelance. He never pushed her to do more. He understood that freelance allowed her time for collecting. Pill boxes at this point, with lids of ornate silver, vivid cloisonné, or porcelain—small, carefully wrought objects of considerable beauty.

Travis didn't collect. He maintained. The roomful of gleaming eighteenth century furniture he inherited from his grandmother was like a pet whose peculiarities they shaped their lives to fit.

"Careful, sweetheart," he would call from the other room when he heard the vacuum cleaner. No scratch, however minor, should mar the flawless finish of a Philadelphia chest, or desk, or Queen Anne chair. He would spend an hour every Saturday dusting and polishing each one, every carved leaf, every claw foot.

A baby would change all that, Lily knew. They'd been trying for more than a year. It was the middle period of trying—sex on schedule, demeaning and awkward postures—everything short of fertility treatments. She dreaded the treatments on account of the hormonal upheaval, the discomfort, the general disturbance they were said to cause. She never mentioned that to him. She didn't need him to point out that pregnancy itself would result in dislocation of considerably longer duration.

"We should be patient," she said when he slid a printout of the newest approach under her coffee cup at breakfast that morning.

On a windy afternoon three weeks later, a paralegal found Travis crumpled on the floor by his desk. The fatal hemorrhage had come from a burst aneurysm in his brain. The doctor said it was caused by an arterial weakness he'd been born with, most likely.

Within two weeks, Lily had put his inherited furniture up for sale. Her collections, too. She was done with all of it. Beautiful surfaces shone everywhere she looked and you couldn't trust a one.

After Emory had been in the little house for a month or so, Lily began cooking dinner for them occasionally, rescuing him from Vienna sausages and canned chili.

It wasn't a relationship, though. It wasn't. Emory was far too damaged by the years of drinking. He would drink anything with an alcohol content—vanilla extract or mouthwash or hair tonic, he said, in the long ago days when that was easily found. His stomach was a mess.

Her meals, however, were nutritious, digestible. Emory put on weight as the months passed. Now, the evenings when they ate together would end with making love in her comfy bed. Comfy love, the kind she seemed designed for. Much safer than the consuming desire of youth she'd never quite allowed. She'd heard too much about the scars it could leave, the wounds beneath that would never quite heal through.

She'd come this far without that kind of pain, at least.

She and Emory were well enough suited, two solitary people, protecting their solitude together. Even when he was gone for a day or several, as he often was, she imagined him alone somewhere with his camera, his pad and pencil, making visual notes for more of his unsettling art. Because his commitment to sobriety remained variable, there'd likely be a quart of vodka nearby, as well. She accepted that.

Early one morning while he was away, Lily set off to investigate an empty house she'd heard about in the distant southwest corner of the county.

The directions she'd been given wound her along miles of intersecting county roads, gravel roads for the most part. Her destination seemed intentionally hidden, far removed from highways and signs of habitation.

The isolation was making her anxious by the time she pulled over and parked. She thought she had the right place, although there was no number on the locked wooden gate. A dirt track led off through hip high grasses into a thicket of hardwoods in full leaf. The fence itself was a joke—three split rails. Set a foot on the lowest, swing the leg over.

The hush as she stood there felt like an open phone line of the kind she'd grown up with—she could sense a person on the other end, listening.

She checked her cell. No service. A chill of vulnerability, familiar enough to any woman, gathered inside her. She could choose either to give in to it and retreat, or keep going. In this case, walking. Peering into the woods on both sides of the track, seeing no signs of life. Not so much as a bird. Ominous, somehow, when birds are silent.

The house was exceptional, though. Her source of information—a woman she knew at the bank—had been right. It was two-story, symmetrical—1850's, probably—and no longer white, more a peeling pied gray. A home for gentry, for planters, fallen on hard times. She could almost hear the swish of long taffeta skirts, smell the smoky, sour remains of a woodfire.

She wanted to look inside—the slats were off the shutters in a few places—but she was afraid to get too close and not only because the front porch might collapse. The house had a complicated presence, and whatever that presence was, it hadn't decided yet what it thought of her.

She would come back and bring Emory.

All that afternoon, she hovered close to her kitchen window, waiting for him to return. He hadn't told her where he was going. He never did. Perhaps he didn't know his destination when he left, merely followed his artistic impulse. She didn't like to think all he had in mind was a multi-day drunk in some run-down motel, away from prying eyes. Her eyes.

She knew the kind of place he'd find. There was a row of small rooms from the fifties a block from the Interstate that she passed whenever she drove to Houston. Its sign had been painted by hand in a hurry, leaving the last three letters, t-e-l, huddled together at the edge, like they were afraid to jump.

It was late the next morning when she caught a flash of reflected light in the vicinity of his house. She'd been standing at the sink for some time, pretending to wash her breakfast dish and mug. She changed into boots for the walk over.

"I've found something fabulous," she told him, when he opened the door. He looked a little out of sorts, like maybe he hadn't slept. "You have to come see. You won't be sorry, I promise."

He didn't smile, but he came, carrying his coffee cup that smelled of bourbon. He never bought bourbon, but never mind.

They parked her car by the gate, like before. At this hour, past noon, the summer heat had risen to the point of discomfort, energizing a variety of insects. The woods swelled and contracted in overlapping crescendos of cicada sound. Lily was sweating openly by the time the building crept into view from behind a row of oak trees.

She knew Emory would take notice of the quatrefoil piercework that remained crisply cut, but he would resonate more truly, as she did, to the splendid desolation that rode on the missing slats of shutters, crumbling porch supports, gaps in the fascia. The delicious *wabi-sabi* of it.

"Isn't the house wonderful, back here where no one would expect it?" She was a little giddy from the pleasure of sharing her find, and she glanced over to see his reaction.

Emory was smiling—rather smugly, she thought.

"What?" she asked.

"I know this house. It was my first job, the summer I finished school," he said. "I'll show you."

They walked around the building into the high grass—there would be ticks, chiggers certainly. The back door was up a few steps from the remains of an herb garden. Tall frowzy stalks of naturalized dill and lamb's ear poked up randomly among the weeds.

"Surely it's locked," she said. The cicadas were so loud in the heat, there'd be no way to hear anyone's approach.

Emory pulled an object out of his pocket, one of those multi-tooled small knives. He bent over the lock and in a moment the door swung open. Where did he learn to do that? She didn't ask.

Inside, the air in the empty rooms was dry and motionless. The only light fell in shafts where a shutter slat had collapsed.

"In here," Emory said. He shone his cell phone flashlight on the painted ceiling. It had been decorated with a delicate precision she would never have expected: Garlands of leaves, a symmetrical classical vase sharply rendered, cascading fruit.

"Miss Maddie Harrison—it belonged to her, then—she let me camp," he said. "Security, she called it. By day I cleaned the painted decoration. It's from the 1860's. And I slept overnight in the back of my truck where the driveway is now. In the dark you couldn't hear cars or people, only the animal sounds, the wild sounds. Hardly any wild around anymore, most places."

His cell light went off.

"It was special," he said from behind her. "The mystery of night away from cities and machines—the silence that comes at you from all sides and beats against your eardrums. Wouldn't you find your heart pounding? Wouldn't you wonder what kind of creature might be circling closer with each pulse?"

"Oh, yes," she whispered. She could feel his bourbon-scented breath on her neck.

"Our civilized protections aren't worth much, really, in that kind of situation," he said. "You can't shoot fear."

The hair on her arms began to rise. "Who owns it, now, Emory? Why is it out here, falling apart?"

"I don't know the answer to that."

At dinner later, he began to chide her. "You're not serious about buying that place, are you?"

She shrugged. "I thought you liked it."

"Even if it had a reasonable price, the cost of moving and repair would keep you in hock to the bank as long as you live. Longer, perhaps." He had a provoking twist to his mouth as he said that.

She reached for his empty plate. "I know you're right," she said, thinking the opposite.

He rocked back in the chair and looked at her. He wasn't wearing his glasses and the pouches under his eyes cast curved shadows on his cheek as he frowned. "You never finish any of your projects, do you, Lily? You're always in the middle. That's a dangerous place. We never see the end of something when we're in the middle of it." He took a long drink of cabernet. "You're not saving these houses of yours, no matter what you think. They'll fall apart the minute you look away."

His fleshed out face was attractive in its red wine flush. Attractive, too, was the sharp edge sheathed beneath the skin of his words. Her blood rose. Her hands shook a little as she carried the plates back to the sink. The dishes and silverware settled against the porcelain surface with a clatter that seemed much too loud. She turned back toward where he slouched boyishly in her most comfortable chair.

A yearning caught at her throat. She wanted it. Desired it with such unexpected intensity she couldn't speak. Not the house, this time. Him. Emory. Sex with Emory in the way she'd thought she'd never feel.

Upheaval. Immolation. Ruin.

He was gone by daylight.

She slept in the next morning, all the way past eight o'clock. Her bed had never been softer, the sheets cool and silken against her skin. She felt well and truly used, a roundness and fullness of use quite unlike anything she remembered feeling before.

She'd poured a second cup of milky coffee and was sitting at the kitchen table in her robe, feeling rosy, when she heard the grinding noise of Emory's tires on the drive between the houses. The wind must have been coming from the north for her to hear it, at all.

She took her cup to the sink, where she could look out in his direction. Unusual of him to leave the place before eleven. She debated for a moment.

Her boots were nearby, though, and she wouldn't need to dress. He'd seen her in far less clothing only hours before in their thrilling new intimacy. Her breath came faster at the memory of his serious face above hers, his steady gaze holding her own—this from a man given to oblique glances in a friendship that, until that moment, offered no conceivable possibility of forward motion.

Her footsteps made almost no sound on the spongy path through the trees. Overhead, wings fluttered. She emerged from the woods into cedar-stippled sunlight.

The front door to the little house stood ajar.

As far as she knew, he went off all the time with the door open, though the mosquitoes would be fierce inside when he returned. He might have been in a hurry, needing coffee or beer from town.

She knocked on the door frame anyway, and, hearing no response, she went in.

The room smelled of his presence and a vaguely chemical odor she associated with acrylic paint. Every surface, however, had been swept clean. No art materials, no liquor bottles. No plate where he might have eaten a quick piece of toast. If she checked the old wardrobe, she would find no clothes. She knew this without looking.

The key to the house rested on the bare wooden table where he often sat sketching. He had left it in the exact center, an old-fashioned key with a circle for thumb and forefinger. The double-toothed bit faced the door like an inverted flag.

He had left no note.

For the next several hours, she berated herself for gullibility, for naiveté, for every shaming deficiency. Her words, spoken out loud, fell back on her like fiery ash as she stripped her bed, ran the sheets and mattress pad on the hottest setting. She was re-making the bed with fresh sheets when she heard someone rap, hard, against the glass in her kitchen door.

Not Emory.

Two men were standing on the stoop, closer to the door than she liked. She opened it, nevertheless. Their expressions, which lacked the feigned agreeableness of salesmen, made compliance necessary.

They were detectives from Austin, they said.

"We're looking for Emory Dahlgren," said the taller of the two men. "There was a residential fire in Westlake Hills night before last. A woman died."

"We understand Mr. Dahlgren had dinner there that

evening," the shorter man added. "Apparently, he was a frequent visitor."

"Several times a month," said his partner.

Lily sat down on a kitchen chair with a thump.

The short one slid into the seat opposite her. "He's not in any trouble at this time, ma'am, but we'd like to know when he left the place. We know he's been staying in one of your houses. You have any idea where we could find him?"

Her eyes met his flat gaze.

The other detective was roaming around the kitchen. Seeing the two unwashed glasses on the counter, the dregs of red wine, the smeary plates in the sink. Working his way over to the bedroom where the silk robe she'd worn lay abandoned on the floor. She'd changed into a loose overblouse, but that, too, seemed inadequate protection against snap judgments.

What went on in there with Emory last night had nothing to do with their inquiry. She could see no reason why these men should finger the shape and texture of her foolishness. No reason for them to know how easily the sudden allure of risk singing in her blood dissolved her meticulously contrived defenses.

She had to answer, though. The detective's unblinking gaze made that clear.

"I suppose he must be in his house next door," she said. "He's usually working at this hour."

And the words came out normally enough, in her ordinary voice. The voice she used to book a manicure, or convince an old farmer to part with his mother's chest of drawers. She spoke each word firmly, too, as though she were referring to someone she knew well, whose habits were predictable and could be relied upon.

As though she had all the breath in the world left to waste on talking.

Intruders

We're too young to live out here. Full time, that is. Not weekenders, not artists, not ranchers. All the ways we are not.

My job, website design, can be done wherever I have bandwidth. The current client sells oilfield tools, downhole probes. Keep it clean, functional, no videos. White space, black font, shiny metal in the pictures. The opposite of excitement.

My attention wanders.

The farmhouse window is old wavy glass. In the pasture, I see undulations, a blur, bifurcating. A dog and a goat. White and black shepherd mix, mid-size; white goat, dirty white—ivory, in card stock.

I giggle.

"What?" Sherm's body sits at a desk, nearby, but his brain roams two miles below the earth's surface, picturing oil sands, shale plays.

"A goat," I say. "Looks like Freud." Dignified. Infinitely more secure than anyone else around here.

I don't mention the dog. Dogs turn up too often near us, dumped, wandering, collarless. Faithfully waiting for the dumbshit owner to come back. Fur all matted, but they're ready to forgive.

I would adopt every one. Nobody would care. Nobody but Sherm. Sherm's opposed to creatures that have to be fed. Moving in, he told me straight out: No animals. OK?

No animals. Right.

Sherm goes out on the porch. The goat lifts its head, its eye on Sherm. A strand of Johnson grass dangles from its lip. The grass disappears into its mouth, like pasta.

The dog's tail starts to wag.

"No," says Sherm.

"No, what?" I am standing beside him.

"Just no. Ignore them." He turns back to his computer, his digits, his multiple displays. The screen door bangs twice behind him.

Next morning, painters arrive, Jesus and Juan. Shy. No eye contact, Jesus especially. No English either, just "okay".

They work. Eat soft tacos, wrapped in crumpled foil. Work. Work some more. The work is excellent.

Sherm's work is gambling. He takes interests in wildcat wells, oil and gas. Lucrative when the well comes in.

If.

If not, dry holes three miles deep, three in five years. Income for the people who drill, build, equip. Zip for Sherm. Minus zip. The investors lose it all. His partners plan one more. Will Sherm commit? His decision. Making it requires concentration. Quiet.

I use earphones, tuned low.

The painters like bouncy Norteño sounds.

Sherm steams, in place. Fidgets.

I respond. "*Señors? Por favor? Musica?*" I make universal signs for less.

"*Si, si, Señora.* O-kay." Their radio goes silent.

An hour passes.

Jesus and Juan are singing. In harmony. Softly. But Sherm's wearing earphones for an analyst's call, so I can let it go.

My client's site is taking shape. My neck is stiff, my butt is numb. I yawn, stretch.

A sudden burst of Spanish. Hooting laughter in the yard.

The goat and dog are back. They gambol. They caper. The goat is a see-saw on wheels. A child's toy. The dog loops around him.

The painters watch them, smiling. Hands hold forgotten brushes.

The next day the dog and goat do not appear. The painters are almost finished, as am I.

A dog barks somewhere nearby. Yelps. A dog in distress.

"Sherm?"

"Somebody's dog is locked out," he says.

All afternoon, the dog cries.

Next morning, I go for my run. A five mile circuit. Pastures, cows, a lake, two creeks, woods. A red-shouldered hawk soars from the top of a telephone pole.

An orange machine chews a trench down the fence line. Matching orange markers march into the woods. Toward us.

I've seen three wells in the area, already. Near Fayetteville, several miles of flexible pipe runs along the side of the road, a giant hose connecting to a new lake, hidden behind a large berm. It holds water pumped from the aquifer.

Weeks ago, I asked Sherm, "What if they put a pipeline through our pasture? Bulldoze our woods for a well pad?"

"What if they don't?" Sherm says. He shuns hypothetical trouble.

Real trouble was losing his family to an ice storm in Colorado, with him driving. Black ice and an eighteen wheeler out of nowhere. He carries the scars on his back, and inside, where they are far more serious.

I'm on the home stretch, now, our own dusty road.

A dog steps out of the underbrush and I stop. A small red setter, a pup. It looks like he's wearing a collar.

I hold out my hand. His tail begins to wag.

Then I notice: The collar is raw flesh. Black at the edges. Adrenaline rushes to my head.

The dog follows me back to the house. I give him water, clean his neck. Blot the sores. Just the tip of his tail wags.

Sherm is anxious. "What are you going to do?"

The tragedy that killed his family was his fault, he believes. The family pets were a warning, dying early, one after the other. Goldfish, then gerbils, hamsters. A cat. Creatures he cared about, all but the goldfish.

I told him that goldfish die for everyone. Small rodents, too.

I name the pup Red.

I make him a bed in the laundry room, soft towels and bedsheets. He looks up at me with the look, soft and grateful, that can never quite be found in a human face. I stroke his silken head.

That night a dog cries in the distance.

Not Red.

In the morning Red and I go walking. No leash. Not with that neck. He won't run off. He won't let me out of his sight.

He trots down the road. That elegant pace of an Irish setter, lovely to see.

He's heading somewhere. The deserted farm across from us. He goes right down the driveway.

I follow.

Trees, a farmhouse. No paint. Porch collapsed on one side. On the other side, a dog, tied with a rope. A terrier mix.

My heart beats in my throat.

A second rope, bitten through. Red was here.

Both dogs left to starve.

I need to set the terrier free. A knife would do, or garden shears.

"Come on, Red," I say.

Red looks at me. His tail half-wags.

He doesn't want to leave.

"Please?"

No deal.

I sprint down the road to our place.

"Uh-uh," says Sherm, at the house. "If you try, he'll bite."

I look at Sherm's square serious face. The sorrow that confines all risk to finance. No heart left for marriage, for another child.

I think of Red. Waiting.

I do a quick search on my computer. Animal shelters. The closest is full. The next one, too. The third will take the shepherd, but they can't pick him up.

Animal control, says Sherm.

I punch in the number.

Sure, they say. No problem. An experienced man will come.

Fine. Great. How long?

"We have someone in the area, should be around twenty minutes."

"Fine."

I begin to pace.

Sherm removes his earphones.

If he tells me to calm down, I will scream.

"I'm sorry," he says. "I really am sorry."

His face, his eyes, tell me he is.

I head back to the farm. I take the car for Red and a piece of chicken. A bribe. He won't want to leave his pal.

No numbers on the gate. How will the rescue guy know where to stop?

I'd better wait out here.

A pickup arrives, pink with dust. A deputy gets out, large, male. He doesn't look at me.

"Thank you for coming," I gush. "I'm taking the red one home. Only the other one is going to the shelter. It's all arranged."

"Yes, ma'am. I'll take care of 'em. You just wait here."

I open the back door of the car for Red and I lean against the fender. I've done a good thing. Red will be sweet company when I run, when Sherm's mind is miles away. It will be good for us to have him around. Even Sherm will see it's the right thing to do.

The silence shatters.

Once. Again.

Two shots.

The woods reverberate.

I cover my ears, but they keep on ringing.

Are You Grieving?

The first time the nation burned she was in graduate school overseas. She watched it on the BBC at night with her shocked roommates, drinking a stiff gin and tonic without ice. On screen, it felt like a documentary from the Second World War. Such violence in her country, in the city—Baltimore—where she went to college. It couldn't really be happening, could it?

So many people died while she was away that year. Martin Luther King. Bobby Kennedy. Her father. She admired Kennedy, and she revered King. She'd been a dot in the mass of marchers on the Mall when he gave his iconic speech. She couldn't hear, but she'd seen it on television many times thereafter.

And, of course, the stubborn truth was that she loved her father.

It was a complex love, because she had confirmed on her last trip home that he was an unrepentant racist. They had argued over civil rights through most of her vacation. He must have been unwell, even then, but she hadn't noticed. She'd been too focused on her own self-congratulatory righteousness.

She thought her stellar reasoning, her legalistic, idealistic argument, would persuade him. Her rhetoric. She thrilled to rhetoric and Dr. King's laid out the world of the future in words that would surely persuade the most resistant Southerner.

She knew nothing.

Her father had been gone, now, for more than fifty years. She herself was older than he was when he died.

And the cities were burning, again, over the murder of a black man. Not a leader, this time. An ordinary man, like most of us. Like so many ordinary unarmed men who had been shot by law enforcement officers. Or throttled. In this case, by a knee. A symbol of historic abuse slipping into present tragedy as bystanders watched. As she watched what cellphones filmed and the symbolic act of oppression acquired blood and sinew and voice. And then lost everything.

She could share her outrage with no one in the flesh, that night. She lived alone, restricted to a couple of country acres in Texas by the virus quarantine. Her husband had been visiting his grandchildren in New York when the edict came down. He could not leave.

She commiserated, but did not protest when he told her. What good would that do? Besides, she was looking forward to the solitude, she realized. A week or two, the way it was when he went on hunting trips. She could snack instead of cooking actual meals.

That had been in March.

It is now June. And the cities are aflame. Tear gas clouds

waft across pavements writhing with microhumans out of Hieronymous Bosch.

She sits in Bob's chair before the wide screen television and watches the street scenes play out. They are just as unreal and far more frightening than any documentary. Or memory.

She speaks with Bob every night on FaceTime, both of them distorted by the curve of the lens and intermittent bandwidth. Versions of themselves, stuttering, moving in jerks, cast platitudes across the distance between them.

Bob is staying in the small guestroom of his son's apartment, a tedious confinement that's growing more burdensome to the son's family—read *wife*—every day. And to Bob, as well.

"I gotta get outa here," he tells her.

She hears the urgency. Bob needs alone time as much as she does. It is one reason their marriage has endured. There is nothing she can do to help him, this time, though.

*

Her father's father, Sam, grew to the age of fourteen on a plantation in South Carolina. Enslaved people worked the farm and served the family, until the War broke out and Sammy went to fight. He never returned home, and those days of cosseted ease and barefoot freedom became trapped in his memory, a Victorian tableau of paradise under glass.

Still, airless, immutable.

In Texas, where Sam settled, her father and his ten siblings were raised with that imaginary place forever mourned. It was as real to them as the image on any screen would be to her, to her grandchildren—images caught by a lens and sent through time, distortions confirmed.

*

She hasn't left their country place in over a month, not even to buy groceries. Deliveries come and she attempts to disinfect them with diluted bleach. The usual disinfectants and sanitizing wipes disappeared from online stores as soon as the pandemic began.

Every morning Bob's old dog and she hobble through the woods to the pond. She watches the dog proceed slowly into the water, submerging his belly. He tongues a couple of noisy swallows before emerging to give himself a thorough shake, as though he has swum a satisfactory distance instead of wading.

They limp back to the house.

These walks in the woods are what have kept her sane during the solitary weeks, the liquid days that come and go more like waves than days, an ebb and flow of light and shadow in which everything changes by minute increments. You can see them if you're looking. Each leaf, each flower, each insect and spider.

Nothing remains the same.

Nothing abides.

Her father choked up at recordings of "Dixie." He refused to listen to "Old Black Joe." It made him too sad, he said.

She saw those reactions like a scrim behind which a

complexity of emotions percolated. "Dixie" stood for something he had never known. "Old Black Joe," too, but what?

Her father had been a thoughtful, somewhat melancholy man. He told stories well, and if prodded would wrap some youthful adventure into an instructive tale, like the time he jumped fences on horseback in defiance of his father, and fell off, onto the barbed wire. He'd been left hanging for half an hour until help came.

In general, though, he resisted questions about the past. His gaze would travel into the middle distance as he began to answer and his words would come slowly, then stop. The lines around his eyes would deepen, and she would feel regret seeping into the space between them. He never explained.

Those songs, "Dixie" and "Joe," were songs of loss, and inauthentic, of course. Sentimental and nostalgic. Perhaps, when he heard them, he thought of his own father and the bereavement they both associated with the Old South, but which had been much closer, in truth, to G.M. Hopkins:

It is Margaret you mourn for.

It is yourself.

How could she expect him to view racial justice clearly, when a distorted memory formed the illusion he was raised on?

At the weekend, protesters thronged the cities in the daytime, and, when night fell, some turned violent. Anger flew through plate glass windows, burst into flames, lugged piles of expensive clothing and equipment over jagged glass, quick-timing down streets that throbbed with masked and unmasked youth.

The president reverted to an alter ego of Bull Conner, spouting the phrases of George Wallace, both long dead. He called out active military to intimidate protesters in our nation's capital.

All happening over and over again on her phone, her tablet, her television screen. Streaming discontent and disinformation Live.

Bob's old dog groans in his sleep on the hard plank floor.

She sips a non-alcoholic beer. Her surviving London roommate, isolating by the North Sea with her family, will be putting on the kettle for morning tea about now.

Bob will be asleep in New York, if the sirens allow it.

She walks to the screen door and listens.

Crickets murmur consolation in the humid air, sweet with day's end. Moths cling to the screen.

No June bugs.

They came and went in February, this year.

Fireflies

It was a higher than average one lane bridge with a superstructure of rusty red metal. The open grid of its decking splintered the water's surface into tiny glittering rectangles that winked on and off as you crossed. Only if you stopped and looked straight down, or looked straight up from below, could you see anything clearly.

Hattie never caught much, but that didn't matter. Fish weren't the reason she came to the creek. She came on account of the slow moving water. Looking at it made her go satiny inside. All the parts of her life that no longer fit fell away, there, under the bridge. She would sit on the sloping bank in the stillness of late afternoon, and watch the shadows change.

In years past, she'd stay on, sometimes, abandoning all her responsibilities. She'd sleep rough, roll up in a sheet or light blanket, right there on the prickly bank. No fire ants back then. She'd get up early, build a fire, cook whatever she could catch. A blue speckled skillet, well worn, did the job. No more cooking, though. Not allowed anymore. But she'd still fall asleep and although she tends to doze most any place now, this is definitely the best sleep, lulled by birds and the hum of insect life in the underbrush.

It's nearly dark when voices overhead awaken her. A girl and a boy. At first, she thinks they're looking for her. Someone always is. She compresses herself into as much of a ball as her stiff joints will allow and suppresses a groan.

"Come on," the boy overhead coaxes. "Nothing's gonna happen. I just want to show you something."

"This place scares me," the girl says.

"I'm here, it'll be fine, I promise. You'll like it."

"I'm wearing heels. I can't walk on this."

"Take 'em off, or I can carry you."

Through the metal grill of the deck Hattie can see slivers of the girl's white leg disappearing into a fold of skirt. A two-inch heel pokes through the grate, and the girl reaches down to free it. It seems that her eyes widen when she sees Hattie, but she doesn't speak.

"Now watch," the boy is saying.

A match flares, followed by the searing sound of other matches lighting.

"Look."

One by one, the tiny flames drift toward the water.

"Fireflies!" the girl says.

"I knew you'd like it," he says, and Hattie sees little slices of bare ankle carved by the grid's dark pattern, and the larger shadow of boots, crowding close.

Of course, their bodies come together. It's why they're here, miles from town. Hattie knows how carefully it's been planned—she remembers the little hints, a daring note slipped into the hand, outside church.

Kissing makes so much noise, a wet snuffling. Then, the scuffing of hard leather soles on metal, labored breathing.

"No!" The girl's voice is sharp. "No, Gerry! Stop it!"

Hattie's own breath comes faster. The girl's feet are off the ground, now, wide apart. He has pinned her against the metal railing, pulled up her skirt. There is something dreamlike in the way her bare feet seem to float untethered. She could scream all night and no one would hear her, no one would come.

Her naked shoulder and lolling breast are visible in the moonlight.

Hattie gropes behind her for the skillet. It's not there, not now, but her hand closes on something. She slings whatever it is forward.

It makes a pitiful thwack.

But enough for Gerry's grip to loosen. For the girl to fall onto the steel surface right above Hattie. Her young features compose themselves clearly now on the other side of the grid. Where her eyes should be, there are Hattie's own eyes, dark, unreadable.

The body never forgets.

And Hattie begins a slow scramble upward. What the effort doesn't take of her breath she releases in a whimper that sounds far away, as though it belongs to someone else.

The girl is trying to cover herself.

Hattie's sparse white hair falls in disarray to her shoulders. Her almost translucent legs, emerging from her nightdress, don't seem substantial enough to hold her upright.

Gerry's face swings toward her, much too close with its sour odor of onions.

The girl stands behind him. She's wearing pants now, blue ones. Hattie can see the color because it isn't dark anymore. Daylight has dissolved the bridge, too, or perhaps not daylight, but a harsh illumination from the round fixture overhead.

"Gerry," the girl is saying.

"Shut up, Rhonda."

"Gerry, please, you're scaring her."

A woman's face, now, replaces Gerry's. No smell, not even the cologne you'd expect.

"Miss Hattie," Rhonda says in that coaxing way they have. "It's okay, Miss Hattie, but you gotta get back in bed, now, honey.

"Come on, sweetheart, take my arm. I'll help you."

Motes

Tillman sat on the porch every morning with coffee in a blue metal cup and he looked at the barn. It was a taller than average barn, made of cypress, stone and tin, with doors on both ends and an open shed down one side where animals had once been fed.

On mornings pearled with moisture, he looked at the barn without his glasses. That lent a soft bulk to the structure that he found pleasing until the blur around it made him uneasy. At that point he would shove the glasses back on his face and go inside to cook an egg.

Although the egg always began impeccably, warm from the chicken house, every morning when he cracked it into the hot skillet, the yolk promptly broke. He would stir the disappointing egg into streaks of white and gold, and eat it on a piece of store-bought bread, folded over.

The white bread his late wife, Marta, had baked could never be folded. If you tried, it would break, and not neatly.

For the last number of years, Marta had liked him to be gone from the house for long hours every morning.

I have things to do, she said, that you wouldn't find interesting.

He had no reason to feel banished. The words themselves were ordinary enough even if the fact of her saying them wasn't. And there was plenty to do around the place. Haying, of course. On good years, several cuttings. He tilled a large plot on the slope behind the house and planted rows of vegetables. Replaced rotten wood with bright new boards. One season, he built a worm fence across the front of the property, making it entirely of scavenged gray cedar. When he finished that, he hunkered down beside it and looked back at the house.

It was the standard Texas farmhouse of the last century, a single story with cypress siding so tough it would barely take a nail. In the low humidity that day it looked as solid as the wooden alphabet blocks children used to play with.

Thinking about those blocks, he pulled an envelope out of the junk mail on the seat of his utility mule. He flattened it across the vehicle's hood and began to sketch with the stub of pencil he used to mark lumber.

He had always doodled—boxes, for the most part, long interlocking skeins of them, snaking along the edge of any handy scrap of paper. The repetition soothed him, the almost predictability of what would come next.

Drawing the house was not too different from doodling. The joins of the roof took a little fiddling, but when he had finished he had drawn something he could recognize. It felt a lot like when he built the tool shed or the fence. The thing he had made stood separate from him, entirely itself, no longer subject to whim or doubt.

In the weeks that followed, he would puzzle his wife by remaining on the tractor after plowing or planting, and he would draw the house where she spent her solitary morning hours. He drew it on smooth paper with a new number 2 pencil.

When he decided to add color, he drove to the crafts store in Bernheim, thirty miles away, for a paint set. He kept expecting the woman at the checkout counter to say something that would reveal his foolishness, but she didn't.

His wife didn't either when he showed her one of his finished pieces. He called it finished, although privately he thought it looked primitive, the kind of thing a child would draw. Marta just made a little breathy sound in her throat when she looked at it. But she didn't actually say anything at all.

*

Marta had never been a talkative person. The world kept changing so fast that she could never find the words to fit. She didn't mind silence, which wasn't so silent, really, when you were paying attention. Out here, the sharp, free call of the meadowlark counted for more than human chatter, anyway.

Often when Tillman left the house in the mornings, she set aside her chores and went for a walk. One day she'd find tall purple-headed thistles sprouted along the fence line; the next day, broad yellow blooms sprang from the fingertips of prickly pear. The creek below was dry, but that didn't stop briars from yearning upwards or poison ivy from coiling its brilliance around the trunk of an oak or pecan. It was as though the spinier or more repellent she found a thing, the more certain it was to flourish. This was a thought to edge around carefully when it came, testing its power to tip her into panic.

She might continue, nevertheless, into the evergreen thicket of yaupon beside the dam where she could hear the flutter of birds building their nests, frantic in their need to reproduce. It was their awful vulnerability—to snakes, to varmints, to wind itself—that sent her hurrying back to the house.

Maybe she thought of the house as protection. Tillman was certainly present, there, even when all she could hear was the rumble of his tractor. Or the rhythmic pop of his nail gun and whine of his saw.

His diligence at these necessary tasks was such that the pictures had come as a shock. All of them the same, and just the house itself without so much as a window or door. They were the kind of thing you expect to find tacked to a classroom wall, along about third grade. It didn't seem normal, somehow, for a grown man.

As the pictures accumulated, her discomfort doubled, and doubled again like bread dough. On the rare occasions when she rode with him to town for supplies, she would point out the ruts in the lane, or the cluster of dead trees near the gate, anything to draw attention away from the buildings they were leaving behind. She was afraid if she did look back, the house would be the way he painted it—a forbidding place, shut up tight and sad.

Why don't you try something different? She asked him one day. Why don't you draw the barn?

Tillman was reorganizing his toolbox, the one he kept handy in the house for quick repairs. He had spread the tools across the kitchen table in order of size and type and was polishing them with a chamois cloth. He kept polishing, as though he hadn't heard.

*

The day, years before, that had changed everything for them began with no more than a forecast of heavy weather. They were living then in a sprawling ranch house on the prairie near the Gulf, raising cattle and growing grain sorghum. The ranch had been in his family for three generations, through the Depression years, two world wars, several hurricanes. It had come down to Tillman unencumbered, 400 acres of griddle flat land he found beautiful.

They had one child, Tami, just turned fourteen, a barrel racer of much promise. She was a compact, muscular girl with quick sure movements and an absence, so far, of the moodiness that both parents expected would arrive with the teen years.

They had been a little afraid of that. Marta's guild circle at the church occasionally received reports of teenage daughters who screamed at their mothers, threw hairbrushes or, once, even a flower vase that left a large gash in her bedroom wall. Those daughters ran off with guitar-playing dropouts, or got pregnant and wouldn't tell the father's name. Not Tami, though. Marta had exulted privately in the good fortune that had provided them with such a fine, even-tempered child. She had taken a bit of pride in the achievement of genes and luck and simple good raising.

The squall that day had been typical enough for the Gulf Coast, bulging up quickly in the heat of a summer afternoon. The darkening sky caused no alarm—there had been frequent storms that season and so far nothing to worry about. Tami was leaving the corral, heading for the barn to put up her horse. She dismounted in her usual fluid motion to push the gate on the old corral open, a heavy gate bigger than she was, with a rusted latch that her father kept meaning to replace.

Marta had been standing at the kitchen sink when a freakish gust flung dirt and debris across the yard. Marta had seen the gate blow back, so slowly in retrospect, so slowly did her daughter fall.

An inch either way and she would have had a bump from its protruding arm. Only a bump.

Left to his own choosing, Tillman would never have gone away from the ranch where his daughter had done her growing up, where the images of her living self ran beside him every day. Marta, though, could not see past the gate he hadn't fixed bursting from Tami's hands, her hat flying, the horse shying.

The ranch sold quickly.

What decided him on this new place was the barn. He had loved it from the beginning, all the life that the previous owners had left behind on its walls and the backs of doors, swept into corners along with odd bits of hay.

During the first weeks after they moved in, he'd found old harnesses, hay hooks, plow points, garlands of rusty trace chains, a cracked wooden wheel.

Once, he reached for a fifty-year-old can of motor oil on a shelf and dislodged a snake skin, four feet long. That made him jump, but still, he liked the idea that snakes had moved in as the human beings had retreated.

Marta found the barn creepy. She could smell animals, she said, not the clean scent of their lives, but the odor of their decay. She required him to dispose of its disintegrating contents. It was the only time he hired someone to do a job on the place that he was capable of doing alone.

The barn sat empty afterwards, and every morning he looked at it over coffee before getting on with his day, the day that Marta shaped as surely as her hands did the dough she molded, pounded, and baked into loaves.

Under a disguise of nagging indigestion, Marta's illness progressed quickly in her sixty-eighth year, a cancer undiagnosed and untreated until too late. The last thing she did before weakness sat her down was to ring the front room with his pictures, each one depicting a farmhouse in a rolling landscape of grass, virtually identical to the pasture outside. He had about thirty by then. She propped them on the floor—at kick height, he thought. But mainly, arranged that way, they made a row of sudden windows at the base of every wall. A person might easily slip through and disappear, with or without meaning to go.

After Marta died, Tillman spent the hours of his former exile wandering from room to room inside the house. His hands knew where the back of every chair would be. But the rooms had acquired a psychic tilt, as though familiarity had been achieved without his personal involvement.

When he tired, he would sit on the closed lid of the toilet and stare at the claw-footed tub. His eyes would slide over and around the sleek curves where he could imagine his wife soaking. It gave him pleasure to think of her like that, the way she had been early in their marriage with her hair long about her shoulders. He would sit there for hours, remembering, and the sunlight would pour over him, as he sat.

Only gradually, as the months passed, did he become aware that the light had dimmed. At first he thought something was wrong with his eyes. Or perhaps the seasonal slope of the sun was the cause, although autumn was still some weeks off.

It was true that he moved more slowly; that he had no heart for the slaughter of rabbits pilfering his garden, or mud daubers drifting from room to room. The long necessity of keeping nature down no longer seemed worth the effort.

When the climbing rose that Marta had planted at the corner of the kitchen porch began to pry off the decorative trim, he made a decision. He would move into the barn.

He bought what he needed in town, a cot, a chair, a cooler for drinks and hot plate for cooking. A piss pot. When he wanted to bathe—which wasn't often—he returned to the house. But he lived in the barn.

He gathered the paintings, dusty by now, from where Marta had left them and carried them to the barn. He set them, gently, in one of the feed troughs, the top one face down. The last one. There would be no more.

He brought his tools from the shed and arranged them on the counter that stretched the length of one wall. He hung his winter coat and hat on a nail by the door. He felt as though he were preparing, for what, exactly, he wasn't sure. But there would be work involved, most likely. He didn't mind waiting to find out what it would be.

Each morning, he lay in the chill dawn air until sunlight struck the window high overhead, frosting a shaft of dust particles that were surely once the living skins of beasts and people. Marta had never understood. She couldn't accept this persistence of what we believe to be lost, so intimately ours in the crowded air we breathe every moment of our lives, even when a breeze is blowing from the north and the stirring on the skin is one of freshness.

Flight

1.

In 1946, snow fields of cotton frosted the flood plain of the Brazos River. For more than a century, the Brazos had been plantation country, and the cotton was still picked by hand, formerly enslaved Africans giving way to brown migrants from Mexico.

The car bumped along one of the narrow dirt roads, barely more than paths, that served the fields. John was driving his dad's old dun-colored Dodge that needed help going into reverse. He used a bottle opener, the kind with a handle, to lever it into the slot.

"Slick," Mac said from the passenger seat.

Mac was boss of this venture. He'd be writing the copy, on the importance of migrants to the Texas economy. More than economics, Mac said. He intended to write about their lives, the families they brought along as they worked and lived in the fields, often in one room shacks built for the purpose of shelter only. If they were lucky.

"How much are they paid?" John asked. A grad student war vet, he was always looking to make a few extra bucks.

"Sufficient," Mac said, when he had thought about it. "A dollar goes a lot further in Mexico."

John understood, then. The families were paid the absolute minimum. Only half a step up from the Africans who'd done the work long before, for no pay at all.

2.

Between the farmhouse and the barn, the yard is lumpy, pockmarked. Some of the holes are neat, cone-shaped as if made with a tool. Tasha reaches for her father's thin elbow as they walk, but he shrugs her off, then stumbles a little.

"Goddamn armadillos," he says.

"Why don't you live trap them?"

"Trap's too heavy to lift with a 'dillo inside."

John had given up killing most critters, as he calls them, by then. He even frees the blue-black mud daubers who drift through the house like tiny aimless drones.

The first time Tasha saw him capture one, she flinched at the angry buzz of the insect inside the plastic cup.

"That's a lot of trouble to go to," she said.

"Letting them go makes me feel good," he said, watching the dauber soar skyward.

Her father had always displayed a charming eccentricity, but his advancing age shifts her perception of it. He's ninety-two, now. A double cancer survivor with heart issues. He hasn't been truly well since her mother, Leila, died.

He called in February. "I could use your help around here for a while," he said, between coughing spasms.

The coughing alarmed her. No denying a person past ninety was old; no denying they wouldn't be alive much longer. Probably. Most likely.

She hadn't spent nearly enough time with either of her parents in the past few years. After they moved to the country, the distance from Houston was enough to preclude casual drop-ins. Her mother had been the one who kept up, by phone mostly. Her father had never been a chatty person.

Tasha agreed to go, of course. She accepted the change like a sinking person grabs at the nearest float—the collapse of her marriage had come so soon after her job at the newspaper vanished.

Gender-traditional describes their routine at the old farmhouse. She'd transcended that years ago with Brad, her husband, but trying to adjust her father's expectations would have been more difficult than just going along.

The arrangement works well enough, too. Tasha straightens the house, does laundry, cooks. John repairs whatever breaks, as long as he can do it from a seated position. He exercises the dog, Mabel, in a battered golf cart he bought off the side of the highway.

On many mornings, while John and Mabel roam the thirty acres, Tasha sits in the kitchen with coffee and her smart phone, travelling the familiar bleakness of her own interior landscape. "Wallowing," John calls it, but she has cause. She expected to lose her job—newspapers had been shedding staff for years. Her husband was another matter.

She blames their rift on the election. Brad hadn't tried to hide his satisfaction over Hillary Clinton's electoral college defeat, a defeat that Tasha took as a repudiation of her own personal and professional existence. All the slights she'd experienced in her career were about to be symbolically purged, and instead they were ratified.

"You're splitting over politics?" her best friend Shana scoffed. "You're insane, sweetie." But how can Shana understand? She's the only colleague over fifty who hasn't been let go. Shana's life remains recognizable.

Whatever happens with Brad—they're just apart, nothing official, yet—Tasha will have to work at more than babysitting her dad. The prospect is daunting. All those laid-off or bought-out journalists competing for a compatible second career. If only she could think of something she actually wants to do. That's easy enough, really—what she wants to do is what she has been doing for the past twenty-five years.

She's still at the kitchen table when her phone buzzes.

"Damnedest thing," comes John's voice, a little static-y. "There's a truck upside down in our creek, over by the bridge. Better call the sheriff. My reception here's iffy."

"Anyone hurt?"

"No sign of a driver. I couldn't get right down to it, though."

The terrain along the creek is steep, a thirty foot drop from the road, more in places. Whoever was driving that truck had a nasty fall.

Her gloom lifts a little.

When the deputies arrive, she walks with them to the site. Mabel, tail wagging, bounces out of the golf cart to greet them. Tasha can see her father listing a few degrees sideways in his seat. He'd been napping, most likely, but now he eases out of the cart.

The truck is one of the smaller ones, Toyota or Kia. The younger deputy has to clamber over a fallen cedar to peer inside. "Nope. Nobody here," he calls up to them.

"Can it have been pushed over the edge?" her father asks, resting on his cane.

The deputy in charge, name of Heinsohn, grunts. "Goin' pretty fast for that. Driver's lucky. Should have broke his neck, landing upside down. Too dry for any tracks, though."

"We'd sure like some idea if there's an injured person holed up in these woods," her father says. "Or a car thief."

"We'll make our report and let you know." Deputy Heinsohn offers his hand and her father shakes it. "Probably you all should stay away from here for a few days. We'll haul the truck out, see what we've got."

"Joyriding teen?" she asks, on the way back to the house in the cart.

"Not much joy by now, I figure." John raises an arm to deflect a yaupon branch.

Mabel sits between them on the seat, her lolling tongue inches from Tasha's face. *What* has the dog been eating? The odor combines notes of animal excrement with hints of rotting leaf-fall. John seems oblivious, his thoughts far away.

In front of the yard gate, he tells her he has to run to town. "Pick up some birdseed, a couple of other things. You need any groceries?"

"Not today." She won't ask what those 'other things' might be. Her father has always ranged widely over regions of private interest she knows nothing about and where she isn't invited to join him. Her mother had been stoic about it. *He needs his thinking space*, she would tell Tasha when the two of them sat down to dinner without him. *He'll be along when he realizes the time.*

After John is gone, driving the ancient Aggie maroon pickup he refuses to replace, she sets about stripping the beds. Nightly, her father pulls up sheets from all four corners as he writhes through whatever dreams assault an old man on multiple medications. Judging from the fine silt trapped in the folds of the sheet, Mabel joined him last night. Tasha hates when the dog does that. Apart from the mess, she's a big animal and the bed is narrow.

One of Tasha's fears is that her father will fall, break a hip or worse. She knows what can happen to the human body when the wrong part of it strikes the ground from even a modest height.

That truck in the creek had plummeted so much farther—the vehicle skidding, flipping, dropping, carrying its driver head first to the ground. Even if he had dangled from a seatbelt, the whip of contact would have thrust the delicate brain material against the skull. It would have jarred the spine. There would have been some kind of injury.

The driver might have crawled out, anyway, stumbled along the parched stream bed that cuts through contiguous properties for miles. Then what?

Surely the authorities are checking nearby farms, urgent care facilities, hospitals. All the loose ends. Tasha detests loose ends.

She sets the ancient washing machine to limp through the load of sheets and pours a cup of coffee. On the glassed-in porch, she opens her laptop.

She'll start with the license plate.

When she comes into the kitchen, later, she finds John building a sandwich out of deli turkey slices, leftover cole slaw and tomato jam. A chilled Heineken foams in a Pilsner glass beside him. No sign of birdseed.

"Dad, does the name T.D. Caldwell ring a bell?"

He extracts a small jar of spicy mustard from the fridge. "Sure. Owns a lot of property around here."

"He's listed as the truck's owner."

"Probably a ranch truck. No way he was driving it. You've been digging, huh?"

She hears a rising note of relief in his voice. "Some," she says. It had felt good to do familiar work, however minimal.

He takes the sandwich over to the kitchen table and begins to eat. Slow and steady. The clock on the wall clicks off seconds, minutes. She opens a container of blueberry yogurt, spoons some into her mouth, scrapes the bottom of the container when it's gone.

While she washes up, he continues to sit. Something is bothering him.

"Are you okay?" She reaches for a tea towel.

"I keep thinking about the driver of that truck, how he felt in mid-air."

She lets his assumption slide. It probably was a guy. "Terrified, I imagine."

"Or, possibly, for a moment, free," he says.

"Free?" She turns toward him.

"I used to imagine it in the war—what being shot down would feel like. The falling part."

"Jesus, Dad."

"Not saying the driver ditched the truck on purpose. There are more certain ways to kill yourself."

Kill yourself? Where did that come from? The connections between her father's thoughts lately are hard to follow. A worrisome change.

She hangs the towel over the oven handle to dry and studies his expression. As usual, it reveals nothing. "Do you have plans for the afternoon?" she asks.

"I want to look up some things at the library," he says.

The nearest library is thirty miles away on a busy two-lane blacktop. The new fracking sites have doubled the traffic on that highway. There'll be oversize tanker trucks and gravel trucks going too fast. She makes a disapproving noise deep in her throat that he ignores.

He gets to his feet. "Texas seems stranger to me every day," he says.

"What do you mean?" He was born in Midland.

He purses his mouth as if something tastes bad, and shrugs.

This was the summer of the new U.S. border policy that separated families of asylum seekers. At first, the news seemed scarcely believable—that in our country officials were removing children—toddlers, too—from the care of their parents and locking everyone up in overcrowded, filthy cages. Some kids were shipped as far away as New York or California.

Tasha imagines a child pulled away from her mother by uniformed strangers. It reminds her of the Holocaust, but those stories had always seemed far removed from her daily existence of fast food and deadlines, and before that, of term papers and worry over whether a particular boy would call. Growing up, she had taken the presence and safety of her parents for granted.

Now the misery is happening nearby. Four or five hours away, driving fast. Why isn't she feeling it more intensely? Something intervenes. Scabs. Scabs accumulated over her lifetime in response to an onslaught of human cruelty. Unavoidable suffering, every day, in the content of the news cycle and of her work. Scabs were a requirement. Is that why the plight of the families at the border feels so distant?

That afternoon, her father brought home books exuding the musty odors of age and lack of use. Locke, Kant, Frederick Douglass. The kind of writing she's never seen him read before. He's usually poring over industry journals and voting his oil patch pocketbook.

"What's this all about?" she asks, when he sets the volumes on the dining room table. She's sure she smells mold.

"We assume freedom has always meant what we think it does," he says. "I'm interested in the history."

Freedom—even this familiar word has changed under Trump. Or maybe it had already changed.

3.

Tasha sleeps most nights with her bedroom window open a crack so she can hear the soothing night sounds.

She wakes this night for no reason she can name. Her phone says it's three-thirty-two—pitch dark outside, as only country dark can be, far from the ambient light of cities.

Except, no. There is a light, stabbing the darkness. Moving purposefully, not bobbing, but wavering from side to side on the unsteady ground, heading from the barn to her father's truck.

A shudder of apprehension propels her out of bed. Using the phone's flashlight, she pads down the hall to her father's room.

Empty.

At a window, she watches the light move around his truck. He must be out there for a reason. She could switch on the floodlight and ask.

Why not?

Her whole life is why not.

Plus, there's an edginess in their connection, now. His unusual behavior. Her own growing anxiety after midnight, when she startles awake, breathless, certain of falling. Sometimes the sensation of falling is so physical she flails. Once she knocked the lamp off the nightstand, smashing the bulb.

This is all new, but then so much is new. She'd been at the paper for twenty-five years. She'd made good friends, and lately watched everyone except Shana depart. Scattered now across the country, linked mainly on Facebook, Instagram.

For twenty-one of those years Brad was nearby, a comforting presence, yes, and a real partner, she had believed. She told him everything personal. A daily reading of her inner atmosphere, her moods and pleasures, successes and sorrows. She thought he reciprocated with his own, until she realized that listening, seeming to understand, didn't imply any kind of agreement.

Still, for a long time she felt supported by a web of interlocking family affection. It was a small family—Brad, her parents, his parents and brothers, all of them living, coupled, at varying distances from the others.

Her mother's illness had been the first wobble. Love aside, Tasha had defined herself in opposition to the woman. She'd concentrated on career, marrying late, making the decision not to have children. Maybe their conflict was generational, an easy explanation. Tasha hadn't wanted to examine the feeling too closely. But Leila's death revealed that the net of family support Tasha relied on was more like the woven fibers of a sweater where one broken strand frees another and another, so that she is left grabbing at whatever's closest, which gives way, too, until every thread releases.

And she plummets.

Only her father remains. Yet here she is in the early morning hours with the inevitability of his loss slicing into her. She thinks of the photograph she saw—of a child wailing at a wire fence. And she is not a child.

Whenever they speak, he seems so lucid, and yet he wanders the house—now the yard—at odd hours. If she were asleep herself, she wouldn't know about it. She wouldn't have to worry how this differs from his history—the "thinking space" her mother spoke of. If it differs.

Confronting him, though, would bring the reality of her concern into solid presence—that he will die before long and she will be left with only the meagre spiritual resources that she herself possesses.

Jobless. Aging. Alone.

The Sheriff's office occupies a low, beige building across from Bernheim's last surviving dairy. Inside the neon-lit interior, an opaque screen separates visitors from the work that goes on.

Tasha gives her name to the officer on duty, a young man with the high and tight haircut that flatters no one.

After ten minutes, Deputy Heinsohn welcomes her into his cubicle. She can tell he's puzzled by her visit. "What can we do for you, ma'am?"

The desk between them is piled with paper in precarious stacks. A child's teddy bear—missing an eye—straddles a box of tissues on a console behind his desk. A family man. She'll try a soft opening.

"I know you've got a lot on your plate, deputy, but we're curious how our case is progressing. Did you happen to talk to Mr. Caldwell, yet—I believe he's the truck's owner?"

"We've talked to the relevant parties," he says, placing both hands on the desk. Loosely curved fingers, not fists, but a barrier between them, nonetheless. "Didn't seem much point to go further. Truck is pretty much totaled."

"I see that, but we're worried about the damage we sustained," she says, although, all in all, it was minimal. A few broken limbs. She needs some kind of wedge to pry loose more details. "Will there be compensation?"

Money often works.

He frowns. "Where are you going with this, ma'am? Is there some new information you'd like to share?"

"We just want to know why a truck ended up in our creek. Do you know who was driving?"

The deputy leans forward. Condescension rises from his smile like the smell of too much bourbon the night before. "Here's the thing, ma'am," he says. "We think somebody took the truck on a joyride and miscalculated that road, probably at night. Maybe inebriated. Damn lucky no one was hurt."

"But how do you know they weren't hurt? You did testing?"

He pushes back his chair. "Ma'am, respectfully, we can't discuss our procedures. Right now, there's no reason to pursue it further. Is there anything else I can do for you?"

Heat shimmies from the asphalt parking lot as she hurries across it. The steering wheel scalds her hands. Such arrogance. Such complacency. Minus her job, she is only an annoying, nosy female, easily dismissed.

A lifetime of patronizing male behavior thuds in her head. The candidate Trump had hulked over Hillary, far too close. Tasha had registered the threat in her stomach and heartbeat. Now, her hands are shaking as she inserts her key, turns it, flips the AC to high. Pushes her face into the flow.

4.

Summer slogs along with ninety-five degree days into September, until one night a big wind from the north blows several hours of heavy rain across them. And the following morning, a Thursday, Tasha wakes up to autumn.

She celebrates by taking Mabel for her morning walk. Her father doesn't object. He has plenty to do, he says. As usual, she has no idea what.

In the woods, a thin layer of new leaves settles over the brown carpet left behind from previous years. Here and there, a few smaller trees are tipped pale gold. The songs of crickets compete in the grassy places.

The land here tries in so many ways to seduce her, flashing silvery seed heads, exhaling cedar-scented freshness tinged with the richness of leaf mold as she strides along.

But her interests—she reminds herself—lie intractably elsewhere, in city things, city people, in the reasons why people behave as they do, and why it is so often contrary to what is good for them. A dominant trait, this human pig-headedness, and she no more knows the reason for it now than she did at twenty.

Up ahead, Mabel stops, nose parsing a scent. When the dog breaks for the creek, Tasha follows. She arrives in time to see the retriever climbing the other bank.

She whistles, sets off up the stream bed, hoping to keep the animal's clanking tags in earshot.

Despite the previous night's rain, the surface, embedded with gravel, isn't muddy. Hardly surprising that the sheriff's men had found no tracks.

On both sides, dead cedars rise tall and straight above the mixed hardwood growth along the bank. The understory that survived the drouth remains thin and thorny with ropes of briar, prickly yaupon. A man's passage would have been difficult, concealment nearly impossible.

About a hundred yards past where Mabel disappeared, Tasha notices a disturbance in the dirt of the bank that is only partially obscured by new leaf-fall. Like something was dragged, or crawled up. Not an alligator.

The bank is too steep for her to climb, but she shoots a picture with her phone.

When she returns to the house, she shows the photo to her father. "Do you think this could be where the driver left the creek?"

John is combing his sparse wet hair after a shower. He grimaces. "Been quite a while since then. No way to know what goes on in these woods at night. Bobcats, deer, coyotes. The rain could have washed away some ground cover."

Tasha grunts, unconvinced.

John slides a freshly ironed khaki Western shirt out of the plastic laundry bag.

"You ever think this might be one to let go?" he asks.

She frowns. "Let go? Why?"

"If it was a kid joyriding, why mess up his life with questions?"

"You're saying I should ignore consequences? He could have killed someone, a passenger, for instance."

"You're not interested in consequences, Tasha. You're tracking a story. I've seen you do it all your adult life. It's not your work anymore."

He hasn't looked at her once. He knows something. "What aren't you telling me, Dad?"

He fumbles with the snap on his cuff. "Maybe it isn't necessary to have all the answers every time," he says.

A surge of heat quickens her heart. As a child, she was always being scolded for too many questions.

"How about you and your truck in the middle of the night? There's a question I haven't asked. What have you been doing out there?"

He closes his eyes for a moment, a slow blink, and turns toward the closet. When he emerges with his hat in his hand, she realizes he has said all he intends to.

Her father has a point, of course. She is chasing this partially out of habit. And the need for distraction, equally strong.

For the past week, each morning at six, she finds his half eaten bowl of cereal in the sink. The congealed contents mean it's been there for hours. Once, there was a frying pan and traces of egg on a plate. When she asked him why so early, he said, "It's as dark at three as at six."

She wondered if he meant the reverse, but she let it pass.

He'd begun confusing days of the week, by then. Sometimes, he'd forget Tuesday's trash collection until she reminded him. Boxes would be piled in the back of the camper on his pickup.

Last year, she would have told Brad about it. He was always fond of her dad. He would have had something consoling to say. She misses that aspect of their marriage most, a kind of trust she thought she could count on. She doesn't trust men easily.

In the sitting room where they keep the TV, the Kavanaugh hearings are underway. She takes a fresh coffee and settles into her father's brown recliner. The old stereotypes from as far back as Anita Hill arrange themselves like surgical tools in front of the Judiciary Committee. Pick one, or several.

Before long, a woman Tasha's age opens her veins on the witness stand and bleeds for the Senators' amusement. Tasha has to leave the room.

On the porch she grips the handrail. Television should provide distance, a screen of security, but it doesn't, anymore. The hurt you witness passes through, unfiltered, made overly real by the telling.

A man drinks too much and presses his larger strength against you. You can do nothing, and he knows it. That hulking body moving toward you, toward your disbelief. As though you, the person, no longer exist.

The man who forced Tasha long ago, who pinned her on the blue sofa until he was done, had a pink boy's face like Kavanaugh. He was big, like Trump. A woman was only a body to them.

Kavanaugh's own testimony is droning through the doorway when her phone vibrates against her thigh. Brad.

She ignores him. His timing is terrible.

He calls again.

Ignore.

She'll have to speak to him before long, but she won't consider going back until he repudiates all things Trump. He hadn't understood in any way the depth of her distress at the election, or at everything that has gone on since.

She clicks off the television, grabs her car keys.

5.

A veteran newsman told her years ago that if you want the pulse of a Texas town, check the local coffee shop. In the course of her work since, she'd crossed many linoleum floors, sat on many stools. Always there was a short order cook in the back and a table by the door where locals gathered every morning. Anything they didn't know wasn't important. The trick was to let them talk.

JavaLatte, in a converted house on a village side street, doesn't look like a traditional Texas café, but it's the closest approximation—and she's sure the coffee will be better.

The place is empty when she goes in, except for a slim red-haired woman behind the counter.

While Tasha waits for her drink, she examines the pictures hanging above the condiments. Early photographs show a smaller town, with few trees and only scattered frame buildings. Her father will have witnessed many of the changes, known some of the people. She wishes he'd talk about that, sometimes.

People don't act the way you expect, though, do they? Brad didn't. She'd never have predicted he'd go for Trump. What is she failing to understand about the people she loves? What else hasn't she noticed?

The proprietor—her name is Helen—slides Tasha's coffee across the counter. Tasha introduces herself.

"Your place is where that truck went in the creek, isn't it?" Helen's expression balances curiosity with caution.

"That's right."

"Funny business."

Tasha shrugs. "The road takes a bad turn there." She sips. The coffee is excellent. "I heard the truck belonged to T.D. Caldwell."

Helen begins washing out the milk jug. "Huh, I'll bet it was the kid. He's in love with that truck."

Tasha sets her mug down. "What kid would that be?"

"Old Romeo Silva's nephew."

"Who's Romeo Silva?"

"Works for Caldwell, foreman I think, or was. I see the kid sometimes at the Mercantile." Helen settles herself on the stool behind the counter, reaches for her own mug. "He comes in to buy those Mexican Cokes they carry. I like 'em myself."

Tasha hasn't drunk a Coke of any kind for twenty years.

Helen reaches for the sugar, stirs in four packets of raw. "Yeah, maybe that's who it was. Old Silva goes to my church, but the kid hasn't been here long. Doesn't speak much English. Too bad about the truck. If it was him driving, I hope he wasn't hurt."

The elements of the narrative Tasha has been struggling to assemble shake themselves into a fresh arrangement. Her father is bound to have seen the boy in town. Realized the connection. He warned her off, too. *Mess up a kid's life*, he said.

She drinks the rest of her coffee without tasting it.

"You wouldn't know where I could find Mr. Silva, would you?"

Helen blinks a couple of times. "I think he's helping Miss Fanny today."

"I wouldn't want to disturb him at work."

"Oh, nobody'll mind. They're over at the church."

The Lutheran church rests in an oasis of shady calm at the south end of the village. She has never stopped to examine it before, the white frame building with its plain Gothic windows and bell tower, set at the end of a narrow lane.

The parking lot is empty, the door locked.

She walks around to the back, hoping for a second door, one that church workers might use. Instead, she discovers an old cemetery framed in pecan trees and ancient oaks. The graves, arranged in tiers, step down to the edge of a bluff. Vertical headstones, slabs and pillars, show their age in roughened edges, mossy dark inscriptions. A few horizontal stones are more recent, but most memorials date from the nineteenth century.

In front of the lowest level of graves the solid ground gives way to a sweep of flat pasture far below, the creek's overflow land, strewn with bales of new hay. Standing above it now, she feels a tingling, almost a yearning to step off, soar over that field as a raptor might. The little town had planned it well, to leave its early citizens poised for flight, to arrange for their eyes that could no longer see, their lungs that could no longer breathe, this eternal expanse of open air and light.

She returns to the car, thinking of her father's shrinking future, the future they face together.

She drums her fingertips on the steering wheel.

She doesn't really need to talk to Silva, does she? What

would she discover or confirm—that a particular boy loved to drive the fallen truck? That everyone in the town knows it? So what?

She has solved her puzzle.

If the boy's here without papers, he is with family, long resident family, well known in the community. Employees of a powerful man. If he were injured, he would be taken care of. No reason to involve law enforcement. Never had been. All those loose ends are none of her business.

She starts the car.

If she goes back to the house, her father will be there. She'll feel obliged to air it out. And because they never do that, and never will, she'd have to admit to herself how much she misses her marriage. Misses Brad.

She should call him. For now, though, she'll drive to Giddings for Mexican food. That will occupy a couple of hours in this long, frustrating day.

When she returns to the house at four o'clock, she finds the note:

> Daughter,
> I've got to run off for a while. Don't worry about me. Thanks for all you've done, but you need to get on with the rest of your life. Do something besides look after your old dad. Remember, I love you.
> —JLC

Run off. Where? To do what?

A rasp of anxiety pushes Tasha into her father's bedroom where nothing looks abandoned. His old suitcase lolls in the corner of the closet. There are no empty hangers.

The surest sign would be his shaving kit. He'd never go anywhere without his pills. But the kit rests in its usual place, and the pills are in it. His shaver sits on the shelf, the way it always has.

Her breath comes faster. Her mouth is dry. *Run off. The rest of her life.* Not reassuring. Not reassuring at all.

Mabel, crouching in the doorway, lets out a muffled whine.

"What? You're hungry?"

Hopeful look, wagging tail.

"Okay, okay."

That means he's been gone awhile. Since he left that morning? He'd had a shower. A shower, two days in a row. He isn't supposed to do that. Aggravates his eczema.

She sets Mabel's pan of kibble on the floor and goes into the anteroom her father uses for a study. Switches on his computer.

The Windows desktop looks orderly. In Word, recent documents include lists of what he's been reading. Page numbers from various books. Notes on the contents. Apparently, in addition to his readings on freedom, he has developed an interest in migrant labor. That's a surprise.

His email confirms only that he has no idea what a spam filter is for.

She notices, then, that the stack of books has disappeared from beside the chair where he reads.

If he's gone to return them, he'd be back by now, wouldn't he? Or maybe he decided to check out more books, do some shopping. New boots, or a shirt. Toothpaste or floss at the drugstore. Ordinary, daily things.

Nothing to do with "running off." But how clear is his thinking?

He has certainly never wandered off before. She thinks of freeway notification signs: *Missing Elderly*.

She'd always thought the term sounded romantic, somehow. Whatever the old people might or might not perceive accurately, they knew enough to flee. To "run off." Her father isn't like that, though. Not yet. Surely.

So, what is she afraid of? What might happen?

Injury, of course. Or, to be honest, suicide. That momentary freedom mid-flight that he mentioned thinking about during the war. How long would momentary be, if it was in fact your last moment? It might last forever, that feeling of freedom.

Imagine that.

She takes a breath, exhales slowly.

Or maybe the note might be just what it looks like. He could have been wanting for weeks to caution her about wasting her life and been unable to do so, face to face.

Maybe she's been wrong about everything, and he'll be back by dinner time.

In the meantime, Mabel needs her afternoon walk. And if he's not home when daylight ebbs, she'll turn on the news to fill the sprawling silence, and she'll wait.

6.

No feeling like it, the two-lane blacktop falling away before him, tumbling over a hill, summoning him across a valley, forward to the place where it disappears. He'd never been in the pilot's seat—only a turret gunner—but he figures flying a plane would feel much the same.

He's sharing the road today with big three-bin tanker trucks, for the most part, carrying frack sand. Sometimes, coming toward him, there are larger rigs, dragging segmented tanks of heavy liquids for disposal or recycling.

They'll be with him awhile as he passes through the Eagle Ford shale on his way south. He'll try to skirt it as much as possible. Probably could have timed his departure better, but the trucks run 24/7, and he prefers to drive in daylight.

Good that Tasha never opened the back of the camper. Door-to-door pickup is what he promised. Soon the question will be door-to-door delivery. Point-to-point. If they let him through.

All he knows about the camps on the border is what the TV cameras show. And rumor. The charity down there is hell for rumor.

Silva gave him a list of what is needed. Toiletries, shoes, clothes, diapers, baby bottles, sealed snack food. Gave him names, also, of a nun and a priest, miles apart, doing the necessary work. The nun runs a relief center on the Ameri-

can side. The priest operates across the border
in Mexico, helping asylum seekers who wait for
entry. Border officials actively discourage Amer-
icans from bringing supplies across. Jail is possible, a Mexican jail, deadly for an old fart like
him. Or the American version, if they catch him
on this side.

Supplies arrive where needed nevertheless,
Silva says, brought through official ports of entry
in private trucks, lubricated by the grasa of holy
lies.

And so, he's here, now, tooling along in his
maroon pickup.

Alone.

Free is how it feels. To be away like this without permission, to leave obligation and routine
behind. Traveling without baggage. Only two-
days' worth of pills, wrapped in Kleenex, tucked
in his shirt pocket. He almost feels as young as
the gawky boy he'd been, setting off for college
at sixteen, oblivious to almost everything the
world intended. He wouldn't have wanted to
know in advance, though, what lay ahead.

How did it happen that Tasha was born knowing all the negatives? Where did she learn to
focus on the worm in the bud?

She'll be upset that he's gone. She thinks he's
losing his marbles. So maybe one or two agates
have shot off. He still has a few left inside the
circle of play.

For example, he's reading the map just fine. No need for that GPS crutch. He has turned off his phone, anyway. He doesn't want to be tracked. The point is for him to do something on his own. Do something—emphasis on do, not on what is done. He hasn't got that far, yet. He has no plan beyond going. Making his delivery. Seeing for himself how the people are treated.

Offering help.

No one is more surprised by this than he is.

Acknowledgments

These stories have appeared, in slightly different form, in the following publications: "Silences," "Drouth," and "Motes," appeared in *Southwest Review*. "A Wall of Bright Dead Feathers," was published in *bosque #9*, in 2019.

"Silences" received the David Nathan Meyerson Prize for Fiction in 2011 and was shortlisted in 2012 for the Kay Cattarulla Award for Best Short Story from the Texas Institute of Letters. "Drouth" received notice among the year's "other distinguished" stories in *Best American Short Stories*, 2015. It is part of the New York Public Library digital collection.

So many friends and associates have given me support and encouragement as I wrestled with the slow emergence of these stories. Among them are Shirley Redwine, the late Lucie Scott Smith, Angelique Jamail, Brenda Leibling-Goldberg, Donna Norquist, Erika Krouse, Sally Arteseros, Lynne Walters, Will Warren and, most of all, my dearly beloved first reader, Leon Hale. I am deeply grateful to you all.

The staff responsible for the Winedale campus of the University of Texas have been endlessly kind in allowing me access to the buildings that house the remarkable decorative work of Rudolph Melchior. I'd like to thank the Briscoe Center at U.T. for assistance with their archives of early life among German-Texans, and James T. Kearney whose fine work on Nassau Plantation helped me better understand the role of slavery in the area. Gloria Hickey is among the Friends of Winedale whose knowledge of the community added to the accuracy of my work. All errors, of course, are mine, alone.

"Are You Grieving" calls upon several lines from "Spring and Fall" by Gerard Manley Hopkins (Penguin Classics, 1985).

Publishers Note